Nell's heart thumped.

She turned. And there he was, his thumbs in his belt loops and a glint in his eye, lean and tough and hot. She was so glad to see him, it made her cross.

"What are you doing here?"

"I came to see you," he said, just the way she'd hoped he would four days ago when he'd brought Laila to the clinic to have her baby.

Four days ago. Four days. Without a phone call.

She lifted her chin. "Why? You finished your story."

Joe nodded, still with that unsettling glint in his eyes. "That's why."

"I don't understand," Nell said.

"You mean you don't remember." He took a step closer, taking up more space and more oxygen than a man had a right to. "I told you that first night. Once I file the story, I don't have any rules against taking you to bed."

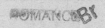

Dear Reader,

Welcome to another month of excitement and romance. Start your reading by letting Ruth Langan be your guide to DEVIL'S COVE in *Cover-Up,* the first title in her new miniseries set in a small town where secrets, scandal and seduction go hand in hand. The next three books will be coming out back to back, so be sure to catch every one of them.

Virginia Kantra tells a tale of *Guilty Secrets* as opposites Joe Reilly, a cynical reporter, and Nell Dolan, a softhearted do-gooder, can't help but attract each other—with wonderfully romantic results. Jenna Mills will send *Shock Waves* through you as psychic Brenna Scott tries to convince federal prosecutor Ethan Carrington that he's in danger. If she can't get him to listen to her, his life—and her heart—will be lost.

Finish the month with a trip to the lands down under, Australia and New Zealand, as three of your favorite writers mix romance and suspense in equal—and irresistible—portions. Melissa James features another of her tough (and wonderful!) Nighthawk heroes in *Dangerous Illusion,* while Frances Housden's heroine has to face down the *Shadows of the Past* in order to find her happily-ever-after. Finally, get set for high-seas adventure as Sienna Rivers meets *Her Passionate Protector* in Laurey Bright's latest.

Don't miss a single one—and be sure to come back next month for more of the best and most exciting romantic reading around, right here in Silhouette Intimate Moments.

Yours,

Leslie J. Wainger
Executive Editor

Please address questions and book requests to:
Silhouette Reader Service
U.S.: 3010 Walden Ave., P.O. Box 1325, Buffalo, NY 14269
Canadian: P.O. Box 609, Fort Erie, Ont. L2A 5X3

Guilty Secrets
VIRGINIA KANTRA

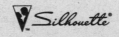

INTIMATE MOMENTS™

Published by Silhouette Books

America's Publisher of Contemporary Romance

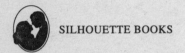 SILHOUETTE BOOKS

ISBN 0-373-27356-8

GUILTY SECRETS

Copyright © 2004 by Virginia Kantra Ritchey

This edition published by arrangement with Harlequin Books S.A.

® and TM are trademarks of Harlequin Books S.A., used under license.
Trademarks indicated with ® are registered in the United States Patent
and Trademark Office, the Canadian Trade Marks Office and in other
countries.

Visit Silhouette at www.eHarlequin.com

Printed in U.S.A.

Books by Virginia Kantra

Silhouette Intimate Moments

The Reforming of Matthew Dunn #894
The Passion of Patrick MacNeill #906
The Comeback of Con MacNeill #983
The Temptation of Sean MacNeill #1032
Mad Dog and Annie #1048
Born To Protect #1100
*All a Man Can Do #1180
*All a Man Can Ask #1197
*All a Man Can Be #1215
Guilty Secrets #1286

*Trouble in Eden

Silhouette Books

Femme Fatale
"End Game"

Family Secrets
Her Beautiful Assassin

VIRGINIA KANTRA

credits her enthusiasm for strong heroes and courageous heroines to a childhood spent devouring fairy tales. A three-time Romance Writers of America RITA® Award finalist, she has won numerous writing awards, including the Golden Heart, Maggie Award, Holt Medallion and *Romantic Times* W.I.S.H. Hero Award.

Virginia is married to her college sweetheart, a musician disguised as the owner of a coffeehouse. They live in Raleigh, North Carolina, with three teenagers, two cats, a dog and various blue-tailed lizards that live under the siding of their home. Her favorite thing to make for dinner? Reservations.

She loves to hear from readers. You can reach her at VirginiaKantra@aol.com or c/o Silhouette Books, 233 Broadway Suite 1001 New York, NY 10279.

To the ones who are living with grace and courage
one day at a time.

Special thanks to my sister Pam
for letting me pick her brain;
to Pam Baustian, Melissa McClone and Judith Stanton;
and, always, to Michael.

Chapter 1

"**M**an here asking for you, Nell," Billie announced as she hustled past the nurses' station.

Eleanor Dolan didn't need a man. She needed six more hours in her day and a forty-percent increase in her operating budget. Or three extra-strength Tylenol and a new pair of orthopedic shoes.

Not that she had a shot at getting any of those things anytime soon. She was used to not getting what she wanted, but she'd learned to make do with what she had. She wasn't settling, exactly. She was... surviving.

Nell sighed and made another note on her patient's medical chart. "Is he a regular?"

The other nurse shook her close-cropped head. This week Billie's hair was an improbable shade of red that glowed against her dark skin. "Nope. But you've got to see this one, Nell. Seriously."

Monday mornings at the free clinic were like Saturday nights in the E.R.—a Saturday night when the moon was full and the Chicago Bulls were losing. "You've got to see this one" could mean anything. AIDS. Asthma. A cut that needed stitching.

"Right," Nell said briskly. "Give him the forms and get him into an examining room. I'll be right there."

She pushed open the door to Exam Eight a few minutes later prepared to find the patient turning blue or bleeding. She wasn't prepared for...

Oh, my.

Nell realized her jaw had dropped and closed her mouth with an audible snap. Billie was right. If you were female and breathing, you had to see this one. Seriously.

He wasn't handsome. Dr. James Fletcher, the volunteer pediatrician, was handsome, his features balanced, his eyes kind, his teeth white and straight.

The man in Exam Eight had sharp, hooded eyes and a smile like a shark. His face was lined, lived in, with enough stubble on his jaw to suit a movie star. Or some homeless drifter. Judging from the quality of his upscale safari jacket, Nell voted for movie star. Although considering the jacket's age, maybe she'd better go with drifter. He looked tough. Streetwise. Dangerous.

Nell distrusted him on sight.

She clutched his chart and forced a smile. "I'm Eleanor Dolan, the nurse-practitioner," she said crisply. "Sorry to keep you waiting, Mr., ah—" She glanced at the sheet clipped to the front of the folder. It was blank, damn it. Somebody should have helped him if he was having trouble filling out the forms.

"Joe," the man supplied. He was still smiling, but his eyes were watchful.

All right, he spoke English. But maybe he was worried about the law or Immigration. Maybe he was embarrassed about his financial situation. Maybe he couldn't read.

She uncapped her pen, determined to help him. That was what she did. Help people.

"Last name?" she prompted.

"Reilly."

She wrote it down. "Do you have insurance, Mr. Reilly?"

He slouched against the examining-room table, his hands shoved in his jacket pockets. "As long as I keep my job, I do."

She mustered her patience and lifted her pen. "I don't know if you're aware of our policy, Mr. Reilly, but the Ark Street Clinic provides medical assistance to people who are uninsured. Your having a job certainly doesn't disqualify you from seeking care. Many of our patients work two or more part-time jobs and earn too much to qualify for Medicaid. But if your employer provides insurance—"

"I work for the *Examiner*," he said.

The *Chicago Examiner* was the city's largest and second-oldest daily newspaper. Nell had been calling and e-mailing both the Metro department and the features editor for months, trying to provoke the kind of publicity that would attract donations to her clinic.

Oh my God.

"You're Joe Reilly," she said.

"Yeah."

"The journalist."

"Guilty."

"You're here to write about the clinic."

Joe kept his hands in his pockets. "That was the idea."

His editor's idea. Not Joe's.

Actually, his editor's idea was for Joe to profile the woman standing in front of him, Eleanor Dolan, the driving force and guiding light of the North Side's Ark Street Free Clinic. The so-called Angel of Ark Street.

Joe thought the idea was hokey and the name probably undeserved. The past year had left him with a jaded view of women and a jaundiced view of the medical profession.

But he could see how the name might have stuck. Eleanor Dolan looked enough like an angel, the kind that showed up in Russian icons flanking the Madonna—pale, blond and severely beautiful. She was even dressed in white, a lab coat, instead of a printed smock like the other nurses wore.

A vain angel? Joe wondered. Not that it mattered. The Dolan woman could dress like the queen of England in white gloves and a blue hat and it wouldn't make her newsworthy.

Although it might be interesting to see what was under that lab coat.

Even if Eleanor Dolan was the angel his boss made her out to be, Joe was no saint. And he was getting mighty tired of self-denial. So he let himself look, appreciating the slope and curve of Dolan's sweater between the open panels of her coat. Very nice.

Of course she caught him staring.

She frowned. "I wasn't expecting you until tomorrow."

He shrugged, enjoying the flash of annoyance in her eyes. "I had some time free today."

"I don't. Monday is our busiest day."

"I noticed."

"Some of our patients wait outside for two hours before the clinic even opens." She must have realized scolding wasn't likely to generate the kind of publicity she wanted, because she softened her tone. "Please come back tomorrow. We'll be fully staffed then, and I can give you a tour."

Joe knew all about official tours. He'd been escorted by experts in Haiti, Kosovo and Baghdad. The skin prickled on the back of his neck.

Which was ridiculous. Eleanor Dolan didn't have anything to hide. She was just anxious to make a good impression.

"That'll be great," Joe said. "In the meantime, any objections if I stick around? Make some general observations, maybe ask a few questions?"

Dolan opened her mouth. Closed it, and tried again. "Not at all. I'll have to ask you to stay in the waiting area, though. To protect our patients' privacy."

Okay, maybe she wanted to make a good impression.

And maybe she was a little bit of a control freak.

"Sure, no problem," Joe said.

And it wasn't, he thought as she led him back to the lounge. He wasn't Ed Bradley from *60 Minutes*. Hell, he wasn't even Joe Reilly, wonder-boy foreign correspondent anymore. He was just Joe Reilly, staff writer, and unless Nurse Dolan was dealing drugs from the clinic waiting room, she had nothing to fear from him.

* * *

Nell regarded the clinic pharmacist in disbelief. "What do you mean, you think we might be missing units from the narcotics closet?"

She heard her voice rising and struggled to contain it. She didn't want to scare the patients.

But Ed Johnson, the pharmacist, flinched. He looked almost ill, slack and pale, his forehead beaded with sweat.

Nell sympathized. She felt sick herself. "How many units?" she asked. "And which drugs are missing?"

Ed rubbed his shiny face with one hand. "I don't know, exactly."

This was bad. Any theft or significant loss of controlled substances had to be reported to the nearest DEA office as well as to the police. But if she didn't even know what was missing…

"When did you take inventory?"

Ed's gaze slid from her. "I was keeping a tally," he mumbled.

"Ed."

At her tone, Lucy Morales, one of the RNs, looked over.

Nell took a deep breath and tried again. "You're supposed to take inventory twice a day."

"I know," Ed said miserably. "But we were busy."

Nell's patience stretched like a rubber tourniquet about to snap. She loved her job. She did. But she was sick of covering for other people's mistakes, tired of making herself responsible for everyone and everything.

Only of course she couldn't yell at poor Ed. He was past retirement age. And he needed this job, needed the poor salary that was all she could afford to pay him.

"All right," Nell said. "I want you to take inventory now and then again before you go home tonight. Let's make sure we have a problem before we start worrying about how we're going to solve it."

She stomped down the hall, feeling the ghosts of her past breathing behind her. The last thing she needed was to make waves with the DEA. Especially with sharp-eyed, smiling reporter, Joe Reilly, cruising around like a shark scenting for blood.

Nell leaned over the counter that separated the office area from the medical aisle. "Hi, Melody. Has Mr. Vacek come in today?" Stanley Vacek was one of her regulars, an elderly man with a thick eastern European accent and a perpetual scowl who suffered from high blood pressure.

Melody King looked up from the computer screen and blinked, her lavender eyelids startling in her pale face. The office manager had long, mousy brown hair and an abused expression. "He was here a while ago. But I think he left."

"He can't leave," Nell said. "He's hypertensive."

"That don't stop him from walking out the door," Billie observed on her way to take the vitals of the patient in Exam Two.

Nell frowned. "But he needed a refill on his medication."

Melody stuck out her lower lip. "I didn't ask him to leave."

"No, of course not," Nell said, automatically reassuring.

"I think he got upset the other guy was asking questions," the office manager said.

Nell's stomach sank. "What other guy?"

·But she knew.

"That Mr. Reilly," Melody said, confirming Nell's fears. "I think Mr. Vacek thought he was from INS or something."

"He's not," Nell said.

"I didn't say *I* thought he was an immigration officer." Melody lowered her voice. "*I* think he's a cop."

Lucy Morales pulled a chart from the stack on the counter. "Are we talking about the guy in the jacket? Because I think he's hot."

Irritation ran under Nell's skin. Why? Because she agreed with Lucy? She pushed the thought away.

"Hot or not, he doesn't have the right to disturb our patients." She marched into the waiting room, relieved to have someone she could yell at without feeling guilty.

Patients filled the lines of chairs. A shrieking toddler flung himself backward off his mother's lap. An elderly woman sat, her lined face passive, her hand clutching her husband's thin arm.

Reilly was folded onto one of the uncomfortable chairs, one long leg stuck out in front of him. He was smiling and talking over the head of a little girl in purple barrettes to her mother, who was smiling and talking back.

Okay, so she couldn't yell.

He'd still scared off grumpy Stanley Vacek. He scared Nell. Until the problem—potential problem—with her drug inventory was resolved, she didn't want him in her clinic. For her patients' well-being, for her own peace of mind, he had to go.

Nell cleared her throat. Reilly looked up.

"I'm sorry. I have to ask you to come back to-morrow."

Reilly straightened slowly. He wasn't a big man, only a few inches taller than Nell's own five feet eight inches, but his physical impact was undeniable. His eyes, a dark, deep blue, were filled with weary humor. Cops' eyes, Nell thought. Priests' eyes. The kind of eyes that invited confidences and promised absolution.

Only she wasn't confessing anything, and she no longer looked for forgiveness from the church. From anyone.

"What's the problem?" Reilly asked.

Nell jerked her head toward the door. Reilly followed her across the room. She felt his gaze on her back like a hand.

She turned to face him, torn between apology and irritation. "You have to leave. You're making my patients nervous."

Reilly glanced back at the child's mother, watching with undisguised curiosity from the row of chairs. "I was just making conversation."

Was she being unfair to him? "You were asking questions."

"So?"

"So, they think you're a cop."

"Not me," he said. "My brother."

Nell nearly groaned.

She liked cops. Most cops. Most of the time, nurses and cops were on the same side of the fence, separated from the public who depended on and distrusted them. They shared the same exhaustion, the same frustration, the same brand of black humor. But at this moment, with Ed Johnson frantically counting units of Vicodin, Meperidine and Oxycodone in the back room, Nell regarded the police with the same deep misgiving she felt toward…well, toward the press.

She moistened her lips. "Your brother is a police officer?"

Reilly nodded.

"Here in Chicago?"

He cocked his head. "Yeah. But we don't talk much, if that's what's worrying you."

She stiffened. "I'm not worried."

"Scared, then."

"I'm not scared."

"Prove it."

"What?"

Reilly shoved his hands in his jacket pockets. "Prove it," he repeated, his gaze steady on her face. "Have dinner with me tonight."

Hello. That came totally out of left field. He'd flirted with that child's mother more than he had with her.

"Why?" Nell asked suspiciously.

He raised both eyebrows. "You need a reason to have dinner?"

"I need a reason to have dinner with you. I don't know you."

"You can get to know me over dinner."

She shook her head, at least as flattered as she was intimidated by his invitation. "Thanks, but—"

"I write a much better story when I'm familiar with my subject."

"I am not your subject."

His eyes laughed at her. "So, we'll talk about your clinic. I'll even bring my notebook."

He stood there, smiling and sure and annoying as

hell. She had to get rid of him without tipping him off or pissing him off.

"Fine," she said abruptly. "I'm out of here at seven."

"Long day," he observed.

"Yes." And then, because she needed to have the last word, she said, "And now it will be a long night."

His smile spread slowly, making the heat bloom in her cheeks.

"We can hope," Reilly said.

She was late.

Nell's bag slapped against her hip as she turned to tug the clinic door closed. Her purse was stuffed with printouts of all the prescription medicines donated by pharmaceutical companies and their reps, all the drugs purchased and all the painkillers dispensed by the pharmacy in the past three months. Tonight she'd crunch the numbers and reassure herself that there were no slipups, no mistakes in the clinic's accounting of controlled substances.

She couldn't afford a mistake.

Not another one.

Reilly was waiting on the sidewalk in front of the clinic, one shoulder propped against the dirty brick. He straightened when he saw her.

"What's wrong?" he asked, his eyes narrowing in concern. Or suspicion.

Nell stitched a smile on her face that would have done justice to a corpse at a wake. "Why would you think something's wrong?"

"That's a reporter's trick," he observed.

She tested the door handle to make sure it was locked. "What?"

"Answering a question with another question." Reilly smiled winningly. "Cops do it, too."

"Nothing's wrong," Nell said. Her bag weighed on her shoulder, heavy as conscience.

"You're late."

"We had a little excitement at the end of the day." She'd spent the past half hour closeted with Ed, painstakingly checking and rechecking his inventory numbers.

Reilly strolled toward her. "What kind of excitement?"

She shrugged. "Our ultrasound machine is on the fritz." That much, at least, was true. "One of our patients has a possible fibroid, and I had to convince her to go to the E.R."

"Is that bad?"

"It is if she decides not to make the trip. Most of our patients aren't poor enough to qualify for Medicaid, but that doesn't mean they can afford a visit to the emergency room." She looked at him pointedly. "We really need new diagnostic equipment."

Reilly stuck his hands in his pockets. "Is this a date or a fund-raising drive?"

"You invited me to dinner to talk about the clinic."

"I invited you to dinner," he agreed. "Do you want a ride or would you rather follow me in your car?"

"I don't have a car," Nell said.

Reilly started walking along the sidewalk. Sauntering, really. "We'll take mine, then."

He was too agreeable. Slippery, Nell thought ominously. And way too confident, the kind of man who equated sharing an after-dinner cup of coffee with after-dinner sex.

She stopped under a street light. ''I don't get into cars with strange men.''

Reilly stopped, too. ''That's going to make getting to the restaurant difficult.''

Nell offered him a crooked smile. She didn't want to alienate him. She just wanted to keep things on her terms. On her turf.

''Not if we walk,'' she said.

He rocked back on his heels, surveying the street, three- and four-story apartments over storefronts protected by iron bars and sliding grills: a used bookstore, a TV repair shop, a thrift store with a baby swing in the window. On the corner, the Greek market had closed for the night, the fruits and vegetables carted inside, the wooden shutters pulled down to the counters.

''You know someplace to eat around here?''

''I know a lot of places,'' she said. ''Do you have a problem with walking?''

He looked at her, his eyes blank, his mouth a tight line. And then he flashed another of his easy smiles.

''Not if we walk slowly. I'm basically a lazy bastard.''

Nell sniffed. She'd been on her feet all day. ''I'll try not to jog.''

''Then lead the way.''

She was very conscious of the grate of his shoes against the concrete, the whisper of her rubber soles. The gutter was littered with last fall's leaves and last week's trash. Bare trees raised black branches to the light. A car prowled by, its stereo thumping. A woman called. A television spilled canned laughter through an open window. By a Dumpster between two buildings was a furtive movement, quickly stilled; something, human or animal, foraging in the dark.

Nell shivered and pulled her cloak tighter.

"What's with the Red Riding Hood getup?" Reilly asked.

"What? Oh." She glanced down at her long red wool and then over at his safari jacket. "Fashion advice from the crocodile hunter?"

"Hey, my jacket's practical. Lots of pockets."

"My cape is practical, too."

"No pockets," he pointed out.

"It's warm."

"So's a down parka."

"Warm and recognizable," she amended.

"Is that important to you? Being recognized?"

She didn't want him to think she was after publicity for herself. Nothing could be further from the truth.

"It can be," she answered carefully. "Sometimes if I'm working late, or I have to go out at night, the cape is useful. Like a uniform."

"Because you might be asked to help somebody."

Nell hesitated. "Yes."

"Or because it keeps you from getting shot at?" he asked, and she stumbled on a crack in the sidewalk.

"Easy," Reilly said, his hand coming up to cup her elbow through the red wool.

"Not usually," Nell muttered.

When she looked over, he was smiling.

Nell tightened her grip on her bag. The printouts inside weighed on her shoulder. She had to be careful what she said around this guy. The sleepy smile was deceptive. The agreeable pose was a lie. The disinterested air was an act.

Whatever she thought of Joe Reilly personally, he was obviously good at his job.

And that made him dangerous.

Chapter 2

The bartender at Flynn's knew Nell by name. He waved her to a booth at the back and drew her a Harps without asking.

Sliding into the booth, Nell watched Reilly lever himself awkwardly onto the dark vinyl bench opposite. His legs bumped the center pedestal. His mouth tightened.

Concern stirred. Purely professional concern. "Are you all right?"

"Fine." He glanced around. "Nice place."

So he didn't want to talk about himself. That made a change from most of the men she knew.

His sharp reporter's gaze took in everything. Flynn's was a neighborhood establishment, with a long polished bar, a wide-planked floor and a wall lined with bottles. Foil shamrocks and limp crepe-paper streamers hung from the TV, week-old relics of St. Patrick's Day. Fiddles and drums played through the speakers. The air was wreathed in cigarette smoke, sharp with the scents of hops and malt, rich with frying potatoes and grilled onions.

Nell's mouth watered. She'd skipped lunch again today. She inhaled, closing her eyes in pure appreciation.

Her pint clinked on the table.

"What'll you have?" the waitress asked Reilly.

"Club soda," he said. "Thanks."

Nell opened her eyes. He wasn't drinking.

Which meant, of course, that he was working.

Which meant that she better pay close attention, or he was going to gobble her up like a side of home fries.

"I'm sure you have questions," she said.

"A couple."

"I left the statistics in my office." Except for the ones in her purse. Stuffed with papers, it burned against her thigh. "But I can give you general information on the demographics of our patient base."

A muscle moved at the corner of Reilly's mouth. "Actually, I was going to ask if you wanted to order now or later."

"Oh." *That* kind of question. Flustered, she scanned the menu. "Fish and chips, please."

Reilly handed both menus to the waitress. "I'll take the steak. Medium rare."

Red meat, Nell thought as the waitress's white blouse disappeared into the darkness at the back of the bar. At least he didn't eat it raw.

"So, what are you doing at the Ark Street Clinic?" Reilly asked.

Penance, Nell thought.

"I see patients," she said. "I also recruit doctors,

hire staff, schedule the nurses, write grant proposals and—''

''This isn't a job interview, Dolan. I didn't ask for your résumé. I want to know what you're doing there.''

Nell set down her pint. There was no way in the world she was confessing the demons that drove her to shark-mouth Reilly, the reporter. But she could certainly talk about the importance of her work.

''Call me Nell,'' she said. There. That sounded friendly and forthcoming. ''The Ark Street clinic provides top-notch care for a segment of the city that would otherwise go untreated. We have a growing immigrant population in our area. More and more employees—especially in low-paying and part-time jobs—aren't getting insurance through their employers. And with the recent budget cuts—''

''Yeah,'' said Reilly. ''I read the flyer. Very nice. What did you do before?''

''I was a trauma nurse.''

''Where?''

''Does it matter?''

''I don't know. Why did you leave? It can't have been the money.''

Nell was stung. Not just by his assumption, but by his attitude. ''How would you know?''

His gaze flicked over her. ''No car. Cheap watch. Old shoes.''

Even though he couldn't possibly see them under the table, Nell curled her feet beneath the bench. He saw too much.

And actually, her job paid pretty well. But she had debts. Some of them were monetary. And the rest... She picked up her pint and took a long swig.

"Can't you accept that some people are motivated by a simple desire to help?" she asked.

He considered that, his long fingers laced on the table in front of him. He had a surgeon's hands, tapered, the nails neatly trimmed. "Nope," he said.

Forget the hands. Nell frowned. "That's a very cynical position to take."

"Realistic," Reilly corrected. He moved his drink aside for the waitress, who set their plates on the table. "Most people are motivated by self-interest, fear or greed," he continued after she left. "And the ones who tell you differently cause most of the world's problems."

Nell stopped with her fork halfway to her mouth, arrested by the discrepancy between his flippant tone and the bitter look in his eyes.

"Spoken like a frustrated idealist," she said.

"Not an idealist. Just frustrated." He flashed her a Big Bad Wolf grin loaded with innuendo.

Nell felt a buzz. Not a beer buzz, either. This was more like sexual static. Cheap thrills. His attitude was completely unacceptable. Too pointed. Too personal. Too sexual. But his persistence was flattering.

She straightened against the high-backed vinyl seat. She had too much at stake to let herself be diverted by the promise or the threat of sex. Even if it had been twenty-two months, five days and…but who was counting?

She made an effort to drag the conversation back to a clinical, professional level.

"You have to admit that there are caring, committed people in the world who do make a difference," she said. "Our volunteers—"

"Don't you believe it," Reilly said. "More harm

is done by zealots, by people with a cause, people with good intentions, people who frigging care, than all the bad guys in the world.''

She sat back. ''Wow. Are you speaking from personal experience here?''

Reilly met her eyes without apology. ''Yes.''

Nell dragged a French fry through the ketchup on her plate. She didn't want to know, she reminded herself. She didn't want to know *him*. But the caretaker in her recognized and responded to the flat echo of his pain.

''Who hurt you?'' she asked softly.

Reilly raised his eyebrows. ''Are you trying to turn this interview around on me?''

Her heartbeat quickened. ''I thought the purpose of this dinner was to get to know one another better.''

He watched her. ''If that's what it takes.''

There was that buzz again, that jolt, that thrill. These were deep waters. And she was about to wade in over her head.

Unless—oh, God, that would be embarrassing— unless she totally misunderstood him.

''For you to get a story,'' she clarified.

''For me to get you into bed.''

Nell caught her breath. Okay, she hadn't misunderstood.

''Gee,'' she said dryly. ''I'm overwhelmed.''

''No, I don't think so,'' he said, studying her with those hooded, knowing eyes. ''You're annoyed. But maybe you're interested, too. Are you interested?''

Interested, offended, tempted, threatened... She wrapped her hands around her cold mug to keep them steady. ''Are you always this blunt?''

He smiled, baring straight, white teeth. ''It's one

of the principles of good journalism. 'Don't waste words.'"

She struggled to swim against the pull of his sexuality, the warm, lazy current in her own blood.

"Doesn't your paper have some kind of restriction against journalists having sex with their subjects?" she asked.

"Probably. If you were underage, or if I put pressure on you to sleep with me so I didn't trash your clinic in my column, that would be a breach of conduct."

Was he serious?

"Are you actually suggesting I have sex with you to get good publicity for the clinic?"

"No." His eyes were bright and very blue. "Would you?"

Would she? Her mind whirled. She'd slept with men for worse reasons. Not recently, but—

"Of course not," she snapped.

Reilly smiled. Satisfied with her answer? Or pleased that he'd finally gotten under her skin?

"Then it's not an issue," he said. "Once I file the story, I don't have any rules against taking you to bed."

Nell sucked in her breath and almost choked on her beer. She should definitely switch to water.

"I do," she said when she could speak. "Have rules, I mean."

His gaze dropped to her hands on the tabletop. "You're not married," he said.

"No."

"But you used to be," Reilly guessed. "To a doctor?"

Nell glared at him. "So?"

The reporter leaned back consideringly. "So you put the jerk through medical school. Right? And then he...what? Wasted your youth? Cut up your credit cards? Broke your heart?"

Worse. Much worse. Her ex-husband, Richard, had ruined her career, violated her trust and smeared her integrity. None of which she was about to explain to a been-there, done-that, wrote-about-it reporter.

"Something like that," Nell said coolly.

"Figures," Reilly said.

She lifted her chin. "Why? Do I strike you as some kind of human doormat?"

"Nope. But your ex was a doctor. I don't like doctors."

Nell smiled ruefully. "I don't like them myself sometimes."

"You have a problem with the doctors at your clinic?" Reilly's tone was easy. His eyes were sharp.

Oh, no. Nell's stomach lurched. This is what happened when you let yourself be drawn along on the tide of sexual attraction. Some lean and hungry reporter swam up and bit off your head.

She was not letting herself be pulled into a discussion of problems at the clinic. Not with her purse beside her, stuffed with the evidence of possible drug diversion. She resisted the urge to pat it, to make sure her lists and printouts stayed safely tucked out of sight.

"Our volunteer physicians are dedicated to our patients' care," she said.

Reilly grinned, making it personal again, undercutting her best professional facade. "Is that the company line?"

"It's the truth," she said stiffly.

"Maybe. Or maybe all you doctors stick together."

They did. Oh, they did. Nell remembered being called into the chief of staff's office after he had discovered Richard's drug addiction. The hospital administrator had been desperate to propose a way to protect his senior anesthesiologist.

And Nell, shaken, guilty, had agreed to…had agreed.

She looked up from her half-eaten French fries to find Reilly still watching her. "I'm not a doctor," she said.

"You dress like one."

Here was her chance to turn the conversation, to steer it back to her work and the clinic.

"I wear the lab coat because patients like it," Nell said. "Nurse practitioners can provide the kind of basic primary care—diagnosing illnesses, treating injuries, prescribing medications—that used to be available only from a physician. But most people are more reassured by a white coat than they are by an explanation of my qualifications."

"So why not go to medical school yourself? Get the credentials to go with the coat?"

"I have credentials," Nell said, more sharply than she intended. "I like being a nurse. And medical school costs money."

"Which you would know, since you put your husband through, right?"

Nell didn't say anything. She couldn't.

"Did you two have kids?"

Enough was enough.

Nell pushed her plate away and leaned her elbows on the table. "You said this wasn't a job interview."

"It's not."

"Really? Because all these personal questions sure sound like you're interviewing someone for a girlfriend position. And I'm not interested in applying."

Reilly sat back and signaled for the check. "Do you mind telling me why?"

"You can't accept I'm simply not attracted to you?"

Unexpectedly, he reached across the table and caught her hand in his. His fingers wrapped around her wrist. His gaze sought hers. Nell forced herself not to pull away, not to show any reaction at all. But he had to see the color that crept into her face. He had to feel her pulse thrum under his touch. His thumb stroked the soft inner skin of her wrist.

He released her abruptly and smiled. "Nope. I won't accept that."

Jerk.

"Fine," Nell said crossly. "There are still those ethical considerations we talked about. You are writing about my clinic. It would be awkward, at the very least, if we became personally involved. But the biggest reason is that my work demands all my energy. I simply don't have time for a relationship."

Not now, when her bag was bulging with data that could destroy her and her clinic.

And not with him. The last person she needed screwing up her it's-all-under-control life was a hardboiled reporter who saw far too much and asked way too many questions.

"That's reasonable," Reilly said.

Some of the tension leached from Nell's shoulders. She even smiled. "I'm glad you agree."

"I didn't say I agree," he corrected. He dropped a

bunch of bills on the waitress's tray. "I said it was reasonable."

The predatory glint in his eye made her nervous.

The March moon was a clear, cold disk in the sky, its white light lost in the orange glare of the street lamps. Frost glittered on the concrete and tinseled the windshields of the cars lining the curb. Nell's breath escaped in puffs as they walked.

And walked.

Joe set his jaw. His ankle had started throbbing before they even reached the restaurant. Ice and elevation, the doctors said. Yeah, right. Like Nell wouldn't have noticed if he'd stuck his foot in her lap during dinner.

He slung an arm around her shoulders for support. She was slight and strong and smelled faintly of disinfectant. Her hair tickled his cheek.

"Warm enough?" he murmured.

"I'm fine," she said crisply, not turning her head. "Put your hands in your pockets if you're cold."

Despite the pain in his ankle, Joe bit back a grin. "Yes, Nurse Dolan."

She shot him a sharp look and kept walking.

Hell. Sweat broke out on his upper lip. He had to slow down.

Joe made a show of digging in his pockets. "Mind if I smoke?"

Nell slowed her steps to match his. "Not if you don't mind my reciting statistics linking smoking to lung cancer, heart disease and emphysema."

"Go right ahead." He stopped. Thank God. Balancing his weight on his left leg, Joe shook out a cigarette. His third today. He cupped the end and lit it, dragging the blessed smoke into his lungs. *Heaven.*

Nell narrowed her eyes at him. "You really should quit."

Joe exhaled slowly, savoring the rush of nicotine. "I'm cutting out one vice at a time, thanks."

"Really?" She arched one eyebrow. "What have you given up today?"

She was teasing. Maybe even flirting. He couldn't tell. But her question howled through his soul like the wind through a ruin.

Joe shivered, shaken by the memories of the past twelve months. His mother's worried eyes. His brothers' bafflement. His boss's frustration.

What had he given up?

Too damn much.

He shook out the match and stumped along, forgetting for a moment to disguise his limp. "I was going to go without sex tonight," he said. "But if you want to change my mind, sweetheart, I—"

Instinct stopped him. Instinct or some habit of observation honed in war zones across Eastern Europe and the Middle East.

Three young toughs loitered in the block ahead of them, beside the line of empty cars. Joe was too far away to make out their gang colors, but he recognized the aggressive confidence in their moves, the casual menace of their posture. Trouble carried itself the same, in Chicago or in Gaza.

Their symbols were anchored on the right: caps tilted, a pocket inside out, a buckle worn to the side. That meant their gang, whatever it was, was affiliated with the Folks nation. Joe tried to recall what his brother Mike had told him about the Folks, back in the days when the Reilly brothers talked easily about everything. More spread out than their rival nation, the People, gangs in the Folks were quick to defend their territory lines.

Automatically, Joe looked for an open business, a bodega, anyplace with lights. Witnesses.

Nothing.

Hell.

He put a hand on Nell's arm, mentally calculating the distance back to Flynn's. He'd never make it. Could she? He registered the exact moment the boys spotted them, saw the nudge and the shove, felt the stirring of their interest like something nasty poked with a stick.

He and Nell should cross the street. Now.

Too late.

The toughs uncoiled from their stoop and sauntered toward them. Two walked abreast, blocking the sidewalk. One slid between the parked cars to the deserted street, cutting off escape in that direction.

Joe felt the anger cruise through his veins. Anger and fear. The taste of it was sour in his mouth. He wasn't carrying a lot of money. He didn't care much about his life. But the woman with him…

He crushed his cigarette underfoot, damning his unsteady balance, and put Nell firmly behind him.

The gang members prowled closer, making no attempt to be silent or subtle. Light gleamed from their chains, their belt buckles, their eyes. Joe shifted his weight to take their attack.

And then Nell's clear voice piped behind him, "Benny? How's your mother? Are her bunions still bothering her?"

The two boys in front of Joe stopped, confused. Nell stepped forward, smiling, and took Joe's arm.

"Benny's mother works in retail sales," she explained. "So she's on her feet all day. She was in a lot of pain when she first came to the clinic."

She smiled again at the taller of the two toughs blocking the sidewalk, holding Joe's arm tight against her breast so he couldn't swing, couldn't move without hurting her. He could feel her heart pounding against his arm.

"How is she?" she asked again, her tone relaxed and solicitous. "Are those new shoes helping?"

The young man looked down at the sidewalk and over at his friends. "Yeah," he said finally. "She's doing okay."

"Good," Nell said. "You tell her to come see me if she has any more problems. She can come after work. We're open until seven Mondays and Thursdays."

The gangbanger shuffled his feet. "Yeah. Okay."

"You'll tell her?" Nell pressed.

The tough standing next to him, the one with the tattoo on his cheek, snickered.

Benny silenced him with a glare. "Yeah. I'll tell her."

Nell nodded. "All right. Good night, then."

She started forward, still hugging Joe's arm so that he had no choice but to fall into step beside her. Pain lanced his ankle every time his foot hit the pavement. He could feel the faint tremor of Nell's body as she pressed against his arm.

But her steps never faltered. In the orange glare of

the streetlights, her red cape gleamed like a military cloak, like an archangel's wings.

No one followed them.

Joe shook his head. It was almost enough to make a man believe in miracles again.

Chapter 3

Melody King turned twenty-four today, and the nurses were throwing her a party on their lunch break. The office manager had had few opportunities to celebrate in her young life, and few people to celebrate with. A runaway at seventeen, an addict at eighteen, pregnant and in rehab at twenty, Melody had come to Nell straight from community college.

Nell had known she was taking a risk in hiring the inexperienced single mother. But, fresh from her own humiliation at the hospital, Nell had been determined to provide the younger woman with a second chance. And today, watching Melody's thin face light in the glow of a single candle, Nell prayed her gamble had paid off.

As Melody cut her cake, Nell kept an eye out the window for the police. After checking and rechecking the lists last night, she'd called them herself this morning. But what would her discovery mean to the nurses crowding around Melody's desk? What would her decision cost her?

"Cake?" offered Billie.

Nell's stomach lurched uneasily. "No, thanks."

"Nice flowers," Lucy Morales said, nodding at the daisy bouquet by Melody's computer. "Who are they from?"

Melody blushed. "Dr. Jim."

James Fletcher, volunteer pediatrician, acknowledged stud muffin and all-around good guy. His offering raised eyebrows and knowing grins around the nurses' circle.

"It's not like that," Melody insisted with quiet dignity. "He's just being nice."

"Bet that's your favorite present, though," teased Lucy.

Nell came to the office manager's rescue. "No, her favorite present is from her *other* admirer. Show them, Melody."

Proudly, Melody showed off the birthday card her three-year-old daughter had made at day care.

"Pretty," Billie approved. "Trevor's nine, and I swear that boy still can't be trusted with scissors."

Billie's nephew Trevor had sickle-cell disease. His mother couldn't afford health insurance, and Billie brought the boy to the clinic for treatment.

While the nurses oohed and aahed over the card, Nell asked quietly, "How's Trevor doing?"

Billie smile was strained. "He's managing. That's all we can hope for, right? We all manage."

A black-and-white police car pulled to the curb by the fire hydrant. Nell's pulse kicked up.

One of the nurses glanced out at the flashing lights. "Wow. This is turning into quite a party."

"I've got it," Nell said.

"If they're cute, offer them some cake," Lucy called.

Nell hurried to open the front door as two officers—solid, uniformed, with matching gaits and haircuts—climbed out of the car and approached.

"How's it going, Nell." The first cop wiped his brow with his forearm before resettling his checkerboard hat. "Heard you had a little problem."

"Hi, Tom." She smiled. One of the beat cops, Tom Dietz had worked with Nell on a domestic-violence awareness program last year. She liked him.

"Nell Dolan," she said, offering her hand to the younger man looming beside him. She didn't remember meeting him before, but his rugged good looks were vaguely familiar. A definite cake candidate. "And you are…?"

The second officer's grip was warm and firm, his smile friendly. "Mike Reilly. Nice to meet you."

Her mouth dried. He couldn't be.

They think you're a cop, she'd said to Joe Reilly yesterday.

Not me. My brother.

Nell's heart banged against her ribs. She could deal with this, she told herself. She could deal with anything.

"Nice to meet you, too," she said faintly as she led them away from Melody's birthday party and back to her office cubicle, crammed in behind a wall of filing cabinets. "I think I know your brother."

"Yeah?" The young cop looked delighted. "Will or Joe?"

Her last hope wheezed and died like a patient taken off the respirator.

"Joe," Nell said. "The reporter?"

Mike Reilly beamed. "That's Joe. He was with the Seventh Marines when they entered Baghdad. Did you read his—"

Tom Dietz rolled his eyes. "When you're done with the stories from the front, Reilly, do you mind if we take a preliminary statement?"

The young man flushed. Nell smiled at him.

Joe Reilly's brother. Oh, dear.

The last thing she wanted compromising her PR efforts was an investigation into drug theft. The last thing she needed complicating an investigation was lousy PR. The police and the press, working together, could piece together a picture of her past that could destroy everything she'd worked to create.

Tom leaned against an overflowing file cabinet and pulled out his notebook. "Why don't you tell us what's missing?"

Nell took a deep breath. "Drugs. I wrote out a list." She fumbled in her pocket and offered it. The page trembled. "Schedule Three and Four painkillers, mostly. Narcotics. Darvon, Vicodin, a lot of Tylenol with codeine... I wrote them all down."

Mike Reilly took the paper and studied it, his face suddenly hard and not so young.

"Any Schedule Twos?" Tom asked.

Methadone, he meant. Morphine. Oxycodone, rapidly becoming the most abused drug on the planet. An eighty mg tablet had a street value of up to eighty dollars.

"We don't keep any methadone in stock." It was a relief to be able to offer some good news. She hadn't done anything *wrong,* Nell reminded herself.

"And we keep such small quantities of Oxycodone that any theft would have been noticed immediately."

Tom wrote that down. "When did you notice the other stuff was missing?"

"Ed Johnson—our pharmacist—suspected a discrepancy in the inventory last night. I checked the supply records and called you this morning."

"Okay. We'll need to talk to him. Who else has access to the pharmacy?"

Nell wiped her hands surreptitiously on her lab coat. This was where things got sticky. "Ed and I are the only ones with keys. Sometimes, when Ed is gone and I'm tied up with a procedure, one of the nurses will come in to get medication for a patient."

"You loan them your keys," Mike Reilly clarified, his voice expressionless. He sounded like his brother.

Nell winced. It was hard to explain how habit and convenience created trust among members of a medical team. Harder to admit, even to herself, that such trust could have been betrayed. "Yes. But they don't have access to the narcotics cabinet."

Tom rubbed his forehead. "They've got the keys."

"The cabinet has a punch lock," Nell explained. "It can only be opened with a three-digit code."

"And who knows the code?" Tom asked.

Fear, bitter as bile, rose in Nell's throat. She swallowed hard.

"Ed," she said steadily. "And me."

Mike Reilly shifted his seat on the edge of her desk. "Could be a tailgater," he said to Tom.

Nell looked at them hopefully. "What's that?"

"Somebody walks by, looks over your shoulder while you're punching in the code," Mike explained. "It's easy enough to pick up."

"You got a security camera on the inside?" Tom asked.

"No," Nell admitted. In the acute-care room, an older woman was moaning, disoriented and in pain. Nell heard Billie's attempts to comfort her, to make her lie still for an exam.

"A larger pharmacy with a walk-in narcotics vault would have a camera monitoring the inside. But we just have the cabinet. And the camera is positioned to record people approaching the pharmacy window from the outside."

"Okay." Tom closed his notebook. "We'll take a look. In the meantime, you might want to change the code sequence on that punch lock."

A crash sounded from across the hall. Billie yelled for help with the restraints. Mike Reilly looked uncomfortable.

"We don't want to keep you," Tom said. "I'll give you a call in a couple of days, do a follow-up."

Nell blinked at him. Surprised. Deflated. "That's it?"

"We'll file a report," Tom assured her. "Let the assignment sergeant know in case your theft fits a pattern in the area. He might send out a detective. But the amounts you're missing... We'll check, but it's not an index crime. Looks to me like you've got a problem with personal use."

Nell went cold.

"Not you, personally," Mike Reilly said. "Just, you know, somebody with access. You didn't notice if the doors or locks were tampered with?"

"No," Nell said faintly. Her heart pounded. Her mind raced. *Somebody with access.* Ed, whom she'd promised a job? Melody, whom she'd promised a sec-

ond chance? A volunteer doctor? A nurse? "Nothing
like that."

"Well, we'll look into it," Tom said. "Want to
show me that security camera? Even with the bad
angle, you might have something on tape."

He sounded doubtful but kind, like a surgeon explaining a patient's chances of surviving a risky operation.

Nell led the way toward the pharmacy feeling
numb. Someone she worked with, someone she
trusted, someone she'd helped was stealing drugs
from the clinic pharmacy. For personal use, Tom had
said.

She turned the corner. Joe Reilly stood in the work
aisle, leaning over the counter to talk to Melody King.

And things teetered from bad and slid to worse.

"Joe?" Mike Reilly sounded pleased, but puzzled.
"What are you doing here?"

Joe pivoted stiffly on one leg.

Nell took a deep breath. She was not going to
panic. Yet.

She forced herself to compare the two men, as if
she could assess the threat to her clinic on the basis
of their family resemblance. They didn't look alike.
Mike Reilly was bigger, blonder, broader than his
brother. Beside him, Joe looked lean and tough and
scruffier than ever. But something—the shape of their
heads, the angle of their jaws, the set of their shoulders—marked them as brothers. And something else,
a weariness, a watchfulness, marked Joe as the older
one.

"Hello, Mike," he said quietly.

"He said he had an appointment," Melody piped up.

Both men ignored her.

"You listening for my car number on your police scanner again?" the cop asked.

If it was a joke it fell flat.

Joe shook his head. "I didn't know you were here. What's going on?"

Tom Dietz pushed up his hat brim with his thumb. "Nothing you need to worry about. Police blotter stuff."

"Yeah, you stick to the big stories," Mike said. "Are you here to see Nell?"

Nell started. She'd told Mike Reilly she knew his brother. But that was all. Had the young officer somehow picked up on the tension between them? Or was he just used to his big brother hitting on every woman that breathed?

I thought the purpose of this dinner was to get to know one another better.

If that's what it takes.

Joe's face was impassive. "I'm here on a story."

Tom looked from Joe to Nell. "What kind of story?"

Nell stepped forward. The less the two Reilly brothers compared notes, the better. And yet something about Joe's careful lack of expression tugged at her heart. "I contacted the *Examiner* to ask if they would send a reporter to profile the clinic. With all the recent budget cuts, we could use the publicity."

Mike's eyes widened. "You're doing a—"

"Feature piece," Joe supplied grimly. "For the Life section. Yeah."

"Oh." Mike shifted his weight, clearly uncomfortable.

Because he'd assumed Joe was having a personal

relationship with his subject? Nell wondered. Or for some other reason?

"Well, that's great," Mike said finally, heartily. "You're lucky," he told Nell. "Joe's a great writer. He won an AP award for his series on the looting of Baghdad, you know."

She hadn't known.

"Nell isn't interested in my résumé," Joe said.

But Mike continued as if his brother hadn't spoken. "After he got hurt, he laced up his boot and kept right on reporting."

Nell felt a flutter of concern. "You were injured?"

"It wasn't a war wound," Joe said. "I fell."

"Some looters pushed him down a hospital stairwell," Mike explained. Nell sucked in a distressed breath. "That didn't stop Joe, though."

Joe thrust his hands into his pockets. "Yes, it did. It just took me a while to wise up to it."

"He was in the hospital for a couple of weeks when he got back," Mike confided. "Getting his ankle patched up."

A couple of *weeks?* For a broken ankle?

Nell glanced at Joe. He was clearly not enjoying this turn of the conversation.

"Sounds serious," she said.

"Tedious," Joe corrected. "I'm fine now."

"You will be when you get that other surgery," his brother said.

"I'm fine," Joe said again, flatly.

A long, loaded look passed between the two men.

Mike snorted. "Yeah. Fine. That's why you're in Chicago writing PR copy for a cut-rate health clinic instead of overseas covering the action."

Nell stiffened at the good-natured insult.

Joe's face didn't reveal any reaction at all.

"O-kay," Tom said. "We're about done here. I'll just have a few words with Ed in the pharmacy and let you folks get back to—"

Writing PR copy for a cut-rate health clinic.

"—your business," Tom finished. "Mike?"

"Gotcha." He said goodbye to his brother, winked at Nell and sauntered after his partner.

"Are you all right?" Nell asked.

Joe's mouth twisted. "Weren't you listening? I'm fine."

That wasn't what his brother had implied, but Nell figured this was a poor time to point that out.

"What happened?" she asked.

"My baby brother just shot his mouth off."

"I didn't mean here. I meant over there."

Joe rocked back and stared down his nose at her. "I thought I was here so you could give me a story."

Nell's heart beat faster. "I will. You go first."

"Everything I have to say I wrote for the paper."

She put her hands on her hips. "Are you really going to make me dig up back issues from a year ago?"

But instead of grinning, Joe shook his head. "Why should you care?"

She was surprised enough to tell the truth. "Because you were hurt, I guess. Because it's my job to observe and to care, and I didn't even notice."

He smiled then, and the sight of all those even, white teeth against his movie-star stubble weakened her knees. "I knew there was a reason I liked you."

She blinked. "What?"

"I get tired of being treated like the walking wounded all the time." He looked directly into her eyes. "I don't want you to see me as one of your patients, Nell."

Her breath clogged. The moment stretched between them, fine and strong as suturing thread.

Until he snapped it by saying, "Unless you'd have sex with me out of pity. I'm okay with that."

Disappointment made her cross. "Are there any circumstances in which you are *not* okay with sex?"

He considered, then shrugged. "Nope. Can't think of any."

Nell drew herself up. His crudeness could be a deliberate attempt to set some distance between them.

Or he could be a jerk. And she was an idiot for imagining that he was something else, that he felt any corresponding connection with her.

"I'll give you that clinic tour now," she said.

That was a close call, Joe thought as he tagged behind Nell to the acute-care room. Her shapeless white lab coat swayed with her walk.

Sex was one thing. Sex was good. Sex dulled the pain for a while.

But the exchange in the hall had forced him to face that Nell Dolan was not a woman he could simply have sex with. She was perceptive and funny and caring as hell.

She wouldn't accept a relationship that was all about sex. She wouldn't let a relationship be all about her. She would want—God help them both—to know about him. And eventually, all the get-to-know-you stuff that usually kicked off a relationship would lead her to figure out that he was hanging on to a job he hated by the edge of his fingernails. And she would demand to know why.

The thought made him shudder.

Better for them both, safer for them both, if he churned out his story and dragged his sorry ass out of here.

"Why do you need all this equipment?" he asked, interrupting her. "Wouldn't your patients who need these kinds of tests be better off going to the hospital in the first place?"

Instead of taking offense, Nell considered his question seriously. "Some of them. But our goal is to identify and treat illnesses before a patient requires a trip to the emergency room. Many of them are afraid to go to the hospital. And most of them can't afford it. Our clinic is actually cost-effective for the community. For every dollar in donations, we can return seven dollars in health care. I have statistics showing…"

Her face was animated. Her eyes were bright with conviction. And every word wiped out his hopes of taking her to bed.

Nell was a do-gooder, a fearless meddler, a tireless fixer-upper. What had she said? *It's my job to observe and to care.* If they got involved, she would want to help him. She would demand to know why he wouldn't help himself.

And he wasn't going there. Not with his doctors. Not with his family. And not with a woman he wanted to take to bed.

Are there any circumstances in which you are not okay with sex?

Yes. When it threatened to become more than sex and jeopardized the barriers he'd set around his soul to survive.

Nell was still talking about clinic costs with the

endearing earnestness of Mother Teresa and the con-
vincing delivery of a used-car salesman. "It's all
about preventive care. A routine patient visit can cost
a hundred and fifty dollars at a private doctor's office.
Using volunteer doctors, we can provide the same ser-
vices for one-fifth the cost. And that includes a lab
test," she added triumphantly. "If you extrapo-
late—"

"Hey, Nell." The big black nurse stuck her head
in the door. Her hair, shaved short and dyed red,
glowed like the fuzz on a tennis ball. "Let me have
your keys a second."

Nell's hand moved easily to her pocket. And then
she stopped. "Where's Ed?"

"At lunch. You've been so busy you lost track of
time." The nurse flicked a glance in Joe's direction.
"Billie Parker," she introduced herself.

Joe was skeptical. Did she really need keys? Or
was she angling for a mention in the paper? "Joe
Reilly," he offered blandly.

She looked him over. "Yeah, I know." She turned
back to Nell. "Anyway, I need some cortisone sam-
ples for the kid in Exam Six. He has a rash in places
you don't want to think about."

Nell moved toward the door. "I'll get them for
you."

"That's okay. I'll just—"

"I really should get them myself," Nell said.

In the field, Joe had developed an ear for a story
and an instinct for survival. And something in her
tone caught his attention as surely as the sound of a
pistol being cocked.

Billie Parker shrugged. "Whatever. When you find
the time. Exam Six." She started to walk out.

"I'll come with you," Nell said. She turned to Joe, her clear blue eyes questioning. A conscientious frown pleated her forehead. He had to stop himself from smoothing it with his thumb. "I have to get back to my patients. Did I give you what you need?"

Not by a long shot, sweetheart, he thought.

But he couldn't ask for what he needed. Not from anyone, and not from her.

He forced a grin. "Are you offering to play doctor, Dolan?"

Her head snapped back as if he'd slapped her. "Not unless you're volunteering to turn your head and cough," she said icily and stalked out.

Chapter 4

It was amazing what kind of crap a writer could produce when he was up against a deadline and had absolutely no feeling for his subject.

Joe scowled at the half page of text displayed on his computer screen. The cursor blinked impatiently at the bottom. *Write. Now. Right now. Write.*

He swore and reached for a cigarette. Every morning he counted them out, three cigarettes, his day's allowance, and placed them carefully in a box in his breast pocket.

The box was empty. The cigarettes were gone.

Joe checked the ashtray on his desk to make sure. Yep, sometime between typing his byline and that last, remarkably bad paragraph citing statistics on America's uninsured, he'd smoked his last cigarette. Exhausted his supply. Reached the end of his resources and his rope.

Maybe he should give up and turn in the piece his

editor expected. Some slop with Nell Dolan as an angel of mercy dispensing hope and drugs to the city's grateful poor. Nurse Practitioner Barbie, with long blond hair and a removable white lab coat.

She would hate that. Joe almost smiled.

But thinking about Nell, undressing Nell, only made him more frustrated in a different way. Physically frustrated. Sexually frustrated.

He reached again for his cigarettes. Hell. Crushing the empty box in his hand, he lofted it across the living room toward the wastebasket.

He missed. *Loser.*

In his front hall, the doorbell rasped like the final buzzer at a Bulls' game.

Joe hobbled across the bare hardwood floor to the door and peered through the security glass at the side. Two men, one in uniform, occupied his front stoop.

Joe yanked open the door. ''What the hell are you doing here?''

His middle brother Will walked in without asking. ''Ma was worried when you bailed on dinner.''

Mike followed, thrusting a round Tupperware container into Joe's hands. ''She sent us with leftovers. Got any beer?''

His family. He loved them, admired them, let them down… And right now, he wanted them to go away. ''No.''

No alcohol. It was something else he was learning to deny himself.

Mike snorted. ''God, now I'm worried about you, too. What about coffee?''

''Instant. And you'll have to make it yourself.''

''Okay. In the pantry, right?'' Without waiting for an answer, Mike snatched back the covered dish and carried it through to the kitchen. A cupboard door banged. A drawer slammed.

With a curse, Joe limped after him.

"You're not walking too good," Will observed behind him. "You hurt your ankle again?"

Joe gritted his teeth. He supposed it was too much to hope Will wouldn't notice. "Nope. Just overdid it the past couple days."

"Is that why you blew off dinner?"

"No. I told Ma. I have a deadline."

"You still have to eat," Will said.

Joe regarded his brother with loathing. "You sound exactly like Ma, you know that?"

Will grinned at him, five feet ten inches of compact, confident Chicago firefighter. "Say that when you're on both feet, paperboy, and I'll take you down."

It was the kind of threat he used to make before the accident. Even with his brother's qualifier—*when you're on both feet*—the taunt improved Joe's mood.

The microwave pinged from the kitchen.

"Dinner's ready," Mike called.

The scent of Mary Reilly's lamb and onions permeated the hall. The house was small, with one bedroom on the ground floor and a couple of others upstairs that Joe had barely seen. Eight months ago, when he bought the place, the layout had been the house's key selling point. He still couldn't negotiate the stairs easily.

Stumping into the kitchen, Joe dug a spoon from the drawer. Will filled a kettle with water. Mike rescued the plastic container of stew from the microwave and slid it across the table.

Joe lowered himself cautiously onto a chair, cup-

ping the Tupperware in one hand. The smell reminded
him of decades of Sunday dinners eaten off his
mother's lace tablecloth in his parents' dining room.
The solid weight of the container in his hand was
warm and comforting.

"Thanks," he said gruffly.

Will lifted one shoulder in a shrug. *No big deal.*

"Mom made us come," said Mike. "She and Pop
are worried you're not getting out enough."

"Oh, like you do," Joe retorted. "You still live in
their basement."

"I like saving money."

"You like Ma doing your laundry," Joe said.

"Yeah, well, a year ago she was emptying your
bedpan and bringing your meals on a tray," Mike
said. "So I don't want to hear it."

An awkward silence fell.

Mike meant well, Joe reminded himself desperately. He always meant well.

But neither of his brothers understood how Joe's
crash-and-burn return from Iraq had crippled him. He
prayed they never did. To lie at the mercy of his doctors, to wake crying in pain, to rely on pills to function and his family for the most basic human needs
had been a devastating comedown.

He was the oldest, the leader, the one who did well
in school. The foreign correspondent, the world ad-
venturer.

Now he was back to eating his mother's leftovers
and fretting over writing a feature on a hole-in-the-
wall clinic.

Will's chair scraped back. He grabbed the whistling
kettle and poured boiling water into two mugs.

"Want some?" he asked Joe, lifting the kettle.

He wanted a drink. He wanted his life back.

He cleared his throat. "Sure. Thanks."

Will snagged another mug from the cupboard and added instant crystals.

"Don't worry about Mom," he said, stirring the coffee. "I told her you weren't getting out because you were finally settling down."

Joe pushed his half-eaten stew away. "And she believed that?"

"She didn't," Mike said, helping himself to one of the mugs and bringing another over to Joe. "But then I told her you were seeing somebody."

Joe didn't "see" women. He had sex with them, to fill the time and dull the pain.

"Yeah?" he asked, almost amused. "Who did you tell her I was—"

Oh, no.

Mike wouldn't. He couldn't.

He had. He was trying not to wriggle like a puppy who'd missed the paper, but it was clear he knew he'd made a mess.

"Nell Dolan," Joe said flatly, answering his own question.

"She was the only one I could think of," Mike said.

"A blond nurse with an Irish surname," Will put in, a gleam in his eyes. "She's perfect. Mom was thrilled."

Nell was perfect, Joe acknowledged. That was her problem. Or rather, it was his.

She would fit too well into his family and into his parents' expectations for their disabled son. She had the idealism and commitment they admired and he had lost. On top of that, she was Irish. Catholic. A caretaker.

She could take care of him.

The thought was as bitter as his brother's coffee and much harder to swallow.

Joe forced himself to take a sip and turned the conversation. "What were you doing there today, anyway? At the clinic."

"Your girlfriend called us in," Mike said. "Somebody's lifting narcotics from the clinic pharmacy."

Joe felt the tickle of interest like a spider on the back of his neck. "Is it serious?"

"Not yet." Mike waggled his eyebrows. "It wouldn't hurt you to keep an eye on things, though."

It could, Joe thought. He didn't want to get involved with Nell or with her clinic. He was going to turn in his fifteen-hundred words and be done with them both.

But as he sat waiting for his brothers to finish their coffee and leave, he couldn't stop thinking this could be the hook, the angle his story needed.

The hell with it.

Frustration bubbled and seethed inside him. Despite the time he'd lost with his brothers' visit, despite his aching ankle and looming deadline, he needed to get out of the house tonight.

He needed a meeting.

The banging woke her.

Nell's head jerked up. She blinked, disoriented, at the scattered pages of the grant proposal spotlit by her desk lamp. She had to finish it tonight. She had to—

Bang. Bang. Bang. Like a garbage can bouncing down a fire escape.

—open the door.

Nell hauled herself to her feet. Her eyes were gritty. Her mouth was fuzzy. Her brain wasn't working at all. If she had any kind of sense, she'd be home at this time of night. If she had any kind of life…

Someone was at the clinic door, pounding hard enough to threaten the glass. Her heart tripped. Trying to get her attention? Or trying to get in?

The panic button was up front, under the registration desk. It hadn't been used in… Nell couldn't remember the last time it had been used.

She hurried down the hall, switching on lights along the way. The Ark Street Free Clinic wasn't the county E.R. Her practice specialized in preventive medicine and family care. Not belligerent drunks or whacked-out junkies or gangbangers who had to be strapped to their gurneys to stop them from finishing in the hospital what they'd started on the streets.

Bang. Bang.

Pulse racing, Nell flipped the entrance lights. A pale face leaped at her from the darkness beyond the glass. Her heart rocketed to her throat.

Joe Reilly?

Dazed, Nell stood with her hand still on the switch plate and her feet rooted to the linoleum. What was he doing here?

He rattled the door in its frame.

Shaken from her surprise, Nell jumped forward to slide back the bolts.

"What is it?" she asked. "What do you want?"

And it better be good, her tone announced. She was

tired. And she still hadn't forgiven him for his "play doctor" crack.

"Not me," he said immediately. "Her."

He turned and reached down to the bundle of rags huddled in the shadow of the building. The bundle gasped and struck his arms away.

Not rags. A woman. A girl, really, her dark eyes huge in her thin face, her hair covered by a plain scarf, her body draped in shawls.

Nell took a step forward. "Help me get her inside."

"I can't," Joe said tersely.

She spared him a brief, assessing glance. "Your ankle?"

"No. She's Muslim. Unless her life is in danger, it's not permitted for me to touch her."

His sensitivity surprised Nell. But she was already bending down, offering her arm to the young woman. "How did you get her here?" she asked over her shoulder.

Joe looked grim. "I convinced her her life was in danger." The girl cried out. And Nell saw what the shadows and the shawls had hidden until now.

"She's pregnant," she said stupidly, staring at the girl's rigid, distended abdomen.

Great diagnosis, Dolan.

"Not for long," said Joe. "She's in labor."

Holy Mary, Mother of God.

Adrenaline rushed through Nell, jolting her fully awake. She wasn't set up for a birth. She hadn't helped deliver a baby since her OB rotation in nursing school.

"Right. All right." Nell supported the girl to her feet with a strong arm around her shoulders. "Come on, sweetie, let's get you inside. I can have an ambulance here in ten minutes.''

''Not good enough,'' Joe said. ''She could have the baby here in five.''

Had she really thought this dolt was sensitive?

''Let's try to be a little more reassuring, okay? She can hear you.'' Nell turned back to the girl, who had the sweet, exotic prettiness of a Princess Jasmine doll. ''What's your name, honey?''

Joe stretched his arm past them to open the door. He smelled like warm male and coffee. Nell would have killed for a cup.

''Her name is Laila Massoud. And she doesn't speak English.''

Oh. Oh, dear.

Nell held Laila as another contraction wracked her swollen body. How many minutes since the last one? ''Then how do you know her name?''

''I picked up a little Farsi in Afghanistan.''

Nell didn't have time to be impressed. She steered the girl down the hall toward the acute-care room. The poor kid was shaking so hard she could barely stand. How had she managed to walk here?

''Ask her how far along she is.''

Joe gave her a disbelieving look. ''I'd say pretty far along.''

''Not the labor,'' Nell snapped. ''The pregnancy. How advanced is her pregnancy?''

Joe said something to the girl, pausing once as if searching for words.

Laila's brown eyes were wide and unfocused as her body contended with the momentous task of birth. But she answered him readily, even holding up her fingers to make sure he understood.

"She thinks thirty-eight weeks," Joe translated. "She's not sure."

Thirty-eight weeks. That meant her baby was full term, its lungs developed enough to cope outside the womb. Assuming the girl could count.

Nell eased Laila up a step so she could perch on the end of the exam table.

"Raise the head," Nell ordered Joe. "Does she have a doctor?"

He hurried to comply. He was limping, Nell noted with the clarity of crisis, clumsier than she'd ever seen him. But he did as she asked, fumbling with the table's controls to adjust its angle.

With one arm around the girl, Nell yanked on the side rail of the bed. Joe saw what she was doing and raised the rail on the other side.

"No doctor," he said. "Her husband is a business student at Illinois Circle campus. They don't have insurance."

Nell was lowering the girl onto her side when her abdomen—her whole body—went rigid. Her nails dug into Nell's supporting arm.

Two minutes, Nell noted with a glance at her watch. She expelled a worried breath. "Where is her husband?"

"He works nights stocking shelves at the Jewel around the corner. Laila was on her way to find him when—"

"Call him," Nell ordered. As soon as the contraction ended, she dashed to the sink to scrub. "There's a phone book under the front desk. And call an ambulance. I have to do an exam."

Joe escaped as she pulled on latex gloves.

With murmurs and gestures, Nell coaxed the la-

boring woman onto her back with her knees bent and
spread apart. Blood and fluid soaked her skirt. Nell
lifted the wet material out of the way as Laila moaned
and writhed. Her vaginal opening bulged.

Nell caught her breath. Okay, baby was on the way.
Head first, which was good. And fast. Not so good.

She flipped the skirt back down as Joe hobbled into
the room.

"I called 911," he announced. "They're sending
an ambulance. And I left a message with the father's
supervisor."

Laila wailed, an indistinguishable stream of words.

"It's all right, sweetie." Nell stroked her leg, calculating the distance to the supply cart. She needed
blankets. Towels. A suction bulb. Cord and scissors.

Joe's face was white. "I have to leave."

Nell glared at him. "Forget it. I need you here to
talk her through this."

"You don't get it. I can't stay. I'm male. She's
Muslim. I can't see her like this."

"So don't look," Nell snapped. "I have things to
do down here. Get up there and talk to her."

He did as she commanded, bending over the head
of the bed, his voice low and questioning. The young
mother-to-be was crying, shaking her head. Joe tried
again, his deep voice patient and almost unspeakably
gentle.

Nell blinked. Who would have guessed shark-
mouth Reilly the reporter could sound like that?

Joe looked up. "Can you put up some kind of
drape?"

Relief flooded Nell. "Absolutely. In the drawer
there." She indicated the supply cart. "Get them all.

We're going to need them to absorb—'' She caught an armload. "Good. Thanks."

She covered Laila with a blanket and draped her from the waist down with a paper sheet, tenting it over her bent knees. Folding a towel, Nell bunched it under the young woman's right hip.

Laila's back arched. The baby's matted head reappeared briefly at her opening. Laila grunted, twisting with strain.

Nell placed her hands above and below the vaginal opening, applying gentle pressure to keep the baby from coming too fast.

"With the next contraction, tell her to take a nice deep breath and hold it."

Joe relayed her instructions, holding his own breath to demonstrate.

Laila nodded, her gaze never leaving his face. She spoke in urgent Farsi.

"She wants to push," Joe told Nell. His eyes were panicked, his voice perfectly calm.

"She can push during the contractions," Nell said. "Exhale and push for a count of ten. Then another breath, exhale and push, for another count of ten. As long as the contraction lasts. Got it?"

"Breathe, push, exhale, count," Joe repeated. "Got it."

But they didn't. The next contraction was bad. Before Joe finished his explanation, it hit Laila like a train, leaving them all gasping and shaken.

There wasn't time to recover before another contraction struck. But Joe kept talking, and doe-eyed Laila exhaled and pushed like a champ.

"Almost there," Nell reported reassuringly. "Almost. She's doing great. Tell her just a few more… Ah."

Laila groaned.

The baby crowned. There was a wrinkled, red forehead. An ear, flattened to the baby's skull.

"Breathe," Nell commanded.

Intent on delivering the baby's head—support, turn, clear the mouth and nose—Nell was barely conscious of Joe's continuous, soothing rumble. She slipped her finger around, checking to make sure the umbilical cord hadn't wrapped around the infant's neck. Gently, she guided the head.

Laila choked out a question. Joe murmured what sounded like encouragement. Nell glanced up. The girl's head bowed almost to her chest. Her neck was corded with strain. One of her slim hands gripped the bed rail, and the other clenched… Not Joe's hand, Nell realized, bemused. They did not touch, this Muslim woman and the Irish reporter. But at some point Joe must have given Laila his handkerchief. She clung to one end like a lifeline, and he squeezed the other.

Nell's heart lurched at the gesture, at the connection, so tender and strange.

The baby rotated. Another contraction delivered the shoulders. Nell cradled the slippery infant in a towel as the rest of its body emerged, wet and raw.

"Is he here? Is he okay?" Joe demanded.

"She's here," Nell corrected. "You have a beautiful baby girl."

Beautiful. Breathing. Alive. Her thin squall needed no translation.

Tears streaked Laila's delicate face as she held out her arms for her baby. Nell's vision blurred. Joe's eyes were suspiciously bright. He murmured something to the new mother, who smiled and nodded through her tears.

Nell melted.

Like she had time for that. She needed to focus on her job, not her suddenly warm and fuzzy feelings for Joe Reilly.

She suctioned the infant's nose and mouth again. She tied a string around the cord before wrapping the baby in a towel. Nell reached over the drape to place her on her mother's stomach, careful not to pull the umbilical cord.

"She should nurse now," Nell told Joe. "To help expel the placenta. You want to get out of here and see what's holding up that ambulance?"

Chapter 5

The ambulance carrying healthy baby, happy mommy and proud but anxious dad rolled away from the curb.

Nell watched the flashing red lights retreat down the street, her adrenaline draining through the soles of her rubber-soled shoes, leaving her tired and empty. Alone.

Okay, not quite alone.

She stole a glance at the man beside her. Joe Reilly stood with his hands in his pockets and his weight on one leg, looking as unshaven and disreputable as ever. But she would never be able to see him the same way again.

Nell understood the bonds that crisis created between members of a medical team. Before she'd been forced out, she'd fought in the front lines of an E.R. She'd laughed at the med techs' bad jokes over bizarre accidents and fought shoulder to shoulder to save the victims of overdoses and heart attacks.

But birth was a miracle. Sharing it with anyone was a moving experience. Sharing it with Joe threatened the barriers she had been so careful to erect between them. His sensitivity and competence caught her off guard. His utter reliability invited her trust. His tenderness melted her heart.

The sudden intimacy created by the birth was unexpected and awkward. As if they'd fallen into bed on their first date and now had to deal with the morning after.

Nell's face heated. She'd made that mistake in the first desperate months after her divorce, and she hadn't felt nearly as warmly toward her partner then as she did toward Joe right now.

She slid another look at him and cleared her throat. Going for casual so he couldn't guess how he affected her.

"Well," she said brightly, "that was exciting."

The lines at the corners of his eyes deepened when he smiled. "You were amazing."

She was suddenly breathless. A reaction to his crinkly good looks? Or his unaccustomed approval?

"I was just doing my job."

"You do it very well."

For once, he didn't sound mocking.

Nell shrugged, uncomfortable with praise. "I couldn't have done anything if you hadn't brought Laila to the clinic. She was lucky you found her."

It was Joe's turn to shrug. "I was in the neighborhood."

"Why?"

Nell's heart beat faster. Did a tiny part of her actually hope he'd answer "to see you"?

"I had a meeting." He didn't elaborate.

She refused to feel disappointed. "Where? This is hardly your neighborhood."

"Our Lady of Hope."

The Catholic church, two blocks away. Nell arched an eyebrow. "You don't strike me as the Knights of Columbus type."

Joe grinned. "You can't see me helping at the Christmas fruit sale in a blazer with a crest sewn on the pocket?"

"No, you seem more like the reporting-from-the-front-wearing-camouflage-with-a-recorder-in-your-pocket type to me."

His smile faded at the edges. "Once, maybe. Not anymore."

"Do you miss it?"

He stared across the street at the grilled and barred windows of the pawnshop, but Nell got the impression he didn't actually see them.

"Yeah," he said finally, quietly. "I do."

"Then why don't you go back?"

He looked at her then, his blue eyes nearly black in the shadows cast by the streetlight. "Kind of hard to ride mules and dodge bullets with a screwed-up ankle."

The nurse in Nell insisted there had to be a medical solution to his problem. Hadn't his brother mentioned an operation? And physical therapy ought to restore partial strength and mobility to his leg.

But the woman in her responded to the controlled frustration in his voice, to the pain she sensed beneath his careless words.

*I don't want you to see me as one of your pa-
tients, Nell.*

So instead of arguing with him, she wrinkled her
nose. "You know, you've just ruined your image. I
pictured you in a Humvee. A Jeep, at least. You rode
mules?"

"We don't use Jeeps anymore, sweetheart. They've
been replaced by Bradley fighting vehicles. When I
was with the Seventh Marines in Iraq, I was in a tank.
In Afghanistan, I was on a mule." He glanced down
the darkened street. "Can I give you a ride home?"

"That depends." She barely recognized that teasing, flirtatious voice as her own. "What kind of transportation are you offering?"

"My car's still parked at the church."

"It's nice of you to offer," she said.

He stepped closer, close enough for her to see the
stubble on his chin and the deep dip of his upper lip,
impossibly soft-looking in his hard face. Her heart
thumped.

"I am not nice," he said.

She didn't believe him. Not after observing his tenderness with Laila.

"Are you warning me, Reilly?"

"I'm being honest."

"Then I'll be honest, too. It's late, I'm wired, I
don't want to wait for a bus, and I would love—"

*To take you home and see if you could make me
forget that my feet hurt and I'm thirty years old and
alone.*

Nell inhaled. Not that honest.

"—a ride home," she said.

He nodded. Did she imagine it, or did his gaze drop
briefly to her mouth?

"You got it."

He waited while she did a hurried cleanup of the acute-care room, turned off the lights and set the security system. It was nearly midnight by the time she locked the front door.

"Ready?" Joe asked, which was a natural question under the circumstances, but her tired mind loaded it with sexual significance. Or maybe that was his voice. He had a great voice, deep and sure, with a hint of a rasp. The kind of voice that could sell expensive whiskey. Life insurance. Ice to Eskimos.

Was she ready?

She hadn't been last night. *I don't get into cars with strange men,* she'd told him, and here she was about to go home with him. About to let him take her home, she amended, which was a different thing. Or it ought to be. She really didn't know him that well yet.

They walked down the sidewalk, and it was just like the night before except the moon was behind the buildings and the buildings were dark. Night in the city. Nell shivered in her red wool cloak and moved closer to Joe.

He was limping. He covered it well, but now that she knew what to look for she could tell.

"What were you doing in Afghanistan?" she asked.

"What?" He sounded preoccupied.

Tough. She was preoccupied, too. She was thinking about sex. Or trying not to think about sex. More specifically, she was trying not to think about how long it had been since she'd last had sex. *Twenty-two months and six days.* So he could answer the damn question.

"You said you learned to speak Farsi in Afghanistan. What were you doing there?"

"Traveling with the Eighty-seventh Infantry."

"On a mule."

He didn't smile. "Sometimes. The country's resources are drained. Their infrastructure's been bombed out of existence. Up in the high mountains, there are communities where the people are almost completely cut off from news. From aid. From health care."

Why had she thought he didn't care? It was obvious from the grimness of his voice that he cared passionately. But she still didn't understand where he was coming from.

"And you went there...searching for terrorists?"

His breath expelled in a pale cloud. "I went there in search of a story. Did you know that in the province of Badakshan, there's only one hospital in a hundred miles that serves women? And a lot of men don't want their wives treated by strangers. Sixty-four percent of the women of child-bearing age die in pregnancy and childbirth. That's more than anywhere else in the world."

"That's terrible," Nell breathed.

"That's news," Joe corrected. They had reached the church. Its spire loomed above them. "I wrote about it for the *Examiner*. And you know what? Nothing I wrote made a damn bit of difference in those people's lives."

"But if you build public awareness..." Nell said.

Joe unlocked the black Range Rover in the parking lot and opened the passenger door for her. Nell thought it was stupid—he was the one who was injured, she was the nurse—but the novelty of having someone else actually trying to take care of her kept her from objecting.

He slid in beside her, maneuvering his left leg carefully into the car. "Don't kid yourself, sweetheart. And don't kid me. You're the public. Do you remember that story?"

"I don't get the paper," she said.

Weak excuse. They both knew it.

"Then I didn't improve your awareness, did I? I did more to help that girl tonight than I did for those other women in three weeks humping over the mountains." He turned the key in the ignition. The engine roared to life. "Where do you live?"

She gave him her address and relaxed into the leather upholstery, enjoying the unfamiliar freedom from thinking about where she was going or how she was getting there. But she was trained to alleviate suffering, and Joe Reilly was hurting. It wasn't just his broken ankle. He was wounded in ways Nell could only guess at. And she couldn't shrug off his pain anymore than she'd been able to shirk her obligations to her mother the Queen of Need or her husband the King of Speed.

She waited until they pulled in front of her apartment before she said, "If you hadn't written that story, you wouldn't speak Farsi. You couldn't have helped Laila. And you wouldn't have been as sensitive to her needs."

Joe shut off the engine and angled his shoulders against the window. He looked very broad and very dark. "I am not sensitive."

Her nerves hummed. She refused to listen to them. "Fine. You're not nice, and you're not sensitive. What are you, Joe?"

"Try 'frustrated,'" he suggested. "Or 'turned on.' And unless you want me to prove it, you'll get out of the car now."

Nell stayed where she was, her heart pounding. "You need a better threat than that to get rid of me, Reilly."

It was a dare. A goad.

And he responded as she knew, as she hoped he would, leaving his post by the window to close the space between them. His arm was hard against her arm. His breath was hot on her cheek. Nell closed her eyes, braced for the sensual assault of his teeth and tongue and felt…the lightest brush of his mouth before he withdrew. She quivered in surprise. He did it again, touch, brush, withdraw, achingly soft, temptingly sweet, seductively gentle.

Her hands curled in her lap. He wasn't supposed to kiss like this. She'd never known anyone who kissed like this, teasing, exploratory kisses that promised as much as they withheld. Maybe back in middle school…

But no teenage boy in the world had this much restraint. Or this much knowledge.

Joe's mouth was firm and hot and clever. Coaxing. When her lips parted, he took the kiss deeper, dragging her unresisting down and down until her head spun and she was breathless and clinging to him. Her fingers flexed on the rough sleeve of his jacket. He covered her hand with his.

"Invite me up," he said against her lips.

She wanted to.

She'd known the man less than two days, and she was ready to risk disease and discovery because he'd been kind and she was lonely.

Well, and because he kissed like the devil.

Nell swallowed. "I could make coffee," she offered.

"Do you want coffee?" he asked, low and amused.

"No," she admitted.

"Neither do I. And before you ask, I don't want a nightcap, either. I don't drink."

Something set off a tiny alarm in her mind, like the warning blip of a heart monitor. But it was hard to focus when every nerve in her body was pinging, bleeping or tingling.

No coffee.

No nightcap.

No pretenses.

Nell shivered. She wasn't ready yet to accept the consequences of her choice. She'd never been any good at asking for what she wanted. She needed some excuse to invite him up.

She moistened her lips. "So, is this part of my interview?"

Interview? What interview?

Joe drew back to study Nell's face in the slanted light of the street lamp. Her smooth blond hair tumbled against the back of his seat. Her eyes were dark and heavy lidded, her mouth swollen and slick. His blood rushed. His groin tightened. She didn't look like an angel anymore. She looked like a siren, one of those women who lured guys onto the rocks and wrecked them.

All these personal questions sure sound like you're interviewing someone for a girlfriend position. And I'm not interested in applying.

Nell had said that last night. Had she changed her mind?

Or was he wrong about her? Could he take her to bed and trust her to understand it was all about sex? It was only about sex. He couldn't afford for it to be anything more.

Except… Genuine liking and respect mixed with his lust and messed with his head. Didn't she deserve something more? She was a nice woman. A nurturing woman. The kind of woman his family wanted him to get involved with so that they didn't have to worry about him anymore.

He must have been silent a really long time. Too long. Because the heat in her eyes shifted, sharpened to another kind of awareness, and she struggled to sit up. Reluctantly, he loosened his hold on her.

"I didn't think," she said. "Is that a problem for you? I mean, if you haven't filed your story yet…"

She trailed off, looking at him with those wide, clear, expectant eyes.

She was talking about the damn newspaper article. She was concerned about his story. She actually cared about his journalistic integrity.

He wanted to laugh. Or smack his head against the steering wheel in frustration.

"I haven't written the story yet. That is, it's written, it's just—"

"Unfinished?" she supplied.

"Crap," he said. "I need an angle. A hook."

Nell frowned. "What do you mean, a hook?"

How had they gone from high-school necking in a parked car to Journalism 101?

Joe sighed and explained. "The story needs something to catch readers' attention. To make them care enough about the subject to keep reading."

Nell ran her fingers through her hair, unconsciously setting herself to rights. "The problem of the uninsured in this country—"

"—is an issue," Joe interrupted wearily. "Not a hook. Nobody wants to read about issues. Nobody cares."

"I care," she insisted.

"Yeah, well, that's what sets you apart from ninety-nine percent of the *Examiner's* target market."

Nell bit her lip. "I don't know anything about writing, but it seems to me you're going about this the wrong way."

"You think?"

She ignored his sarcasm. "Maybe instead of trying to come up with something that would appeal to some nameless, faceless majority of readers, you should figure out what gets you excited about your story. What makes you care?"

He was so not going there. "You mean, besides the fact that if I miss my deadline my editor's going to be really pissed?"

Nell's earnest gaze never wavered. "Yes. Besides that."

Joe shook his head. He couldn't do what she was asking. He couldn't be the man she wanted or the reporter this story deserved.

"You've got the wrong guy, sweetheart. I don't do caring."

"I don't accept that. You cared about Laila."

"That was different," he objected automatically.

"Different, how?"

"Different *different*." The words burst out of him.

''The kid needed help. For God's sake, you don't ignore a woman who's having a baby on the street.''

And that was it, Joe realized. There was his hook. All the things that had compelled him to get involved with the young Muslim woman would sway his readers, too. Laila's labor and delivery had everything that made a great news story: personal drama, political relevance, urgency, action, even a happy ending.

Would she agree to let him take her picture for the paper?

Nell sat watching him, her smile suspiciously smug. ''No, you don't, do you?''

She undid her seat belt. Leaning forward, she kissed him warmly, briefly on the mouth.

''Good luck working on your story,'' she said, and let herself out of his car.

Joe watched as his chance for sexual release went up the walk with quick, determined strides.

Good luck working on your story?

He didn't want to work on his story, damn it. He wanted Nell.

He watched her unlock the door to her apartment building and close it firmly behind her.

On the other hand, he supposed he could work on the story. He sure as hell didn't have anything better to do with his night. Not anymore.

Nell was disgruntled.

Not because she expected Joe Reilly to call, she assured herself as she wrote out a prescription for Stanley Vacek in Exam Five. It wasn't as if they were seeing each other. Participating in a messy birth and sharing a few relatively innocent kisses in the front seat of his Range Rover did not constitute a commitment. Or even a date.

He didn't owe her anything. She didn't expect anything. If you expected things from people, they only let you down. Nell had learned early in life that if she wanted cupcakes for the class on her birthday, she'd better bake them herself. If she wanted flowers on her anniversary, she'd better buy them herself. And if she wanted soft, searing kisses from a man who made her pulse pound...

Scowling, she added a beta-blocker to Mr. Vacek's thiazide-typed diuretic and clipped both prescriptions to the top of his chart.

Face it. Joe hadn't called in four days. Obviously the kisses that left her distracted and hungry for more hadn't had the same effect on him. From the easy way he'd invited himself up to her apartment, she suspected he probably kissed women all the time. Women who didn't end their evenings together by wishing him luck with his work while they—the women—went to bed alone.

Nell delivered the prescriptions to Mr. Vacek in Exam Five along with a recipe for vegetable soup.

Vacek scowled at her like an unhappy garden gnome. "I don't cook."

"It wouldn't hurt you to learn," Nell said. He needed something to occupy his time besides visits to the clinic. "And it would help if you added some vegetables to your diet."

He sniffed, but he took the recipe.

Nell went out to the flow board by the nurses' station to check on her next appointment. Taped to the wall was the front page of yesterday's Life section.

Delivering Hope on the North Side, the headline read. The byline read, Joe Reilly.

Nell had read the story the day before, but she paused anyway to enjoy the photo. Right there above the fold, a smiling Laila Massoud cradled her baby to her breast.

"Looking good," Billie said on her way to draw labs from the diabetic in Exam Four.

Nell wasn't sure if the other nurse was referring to Laila or the clinic, but she nodded in agreement. "Donations should go up."

The piece was a sensitive chronicle of the day-to-day hopes and struggles of student Arif and his non-English-speaking wife in the wake of 9/11. The two had married over their families' objections and moved to Chicago a year ago. Joe had used the birth of their daughter as a touching symbol of the new life the young couple longed for. It wasn't the PR piece Nell had sought, but there was a nice plug for the Ark Street Free Clinic in the sidebar. Joe had done a good job.

And she would tell him so if she ever heard from him again.

Billie still lingered, her usually cheerful face troubled.

Nell dragged her mind from Joe Reilly's kisses, his article and his silence and asked, "Is anything wrong?"

"It's Trevor," said Billie. "He's having another episode."

In sickle-cell patients, defective blood cells could block the blood vessels, causing bouts of pain that might last for days. Or weeks.

"Poor kid. I'm sorry," Nell said. "What does Dr. Jim say?"

"What can he say? He told him to drink a lot of water, stay warm and avoid getting tired." Billie snorted. "Like the boy can get tired when he can't even get out of bed."

Nell winced in sympathy. "Did you ask about putting him on hydroxyurea? It's not a cure, but—"

Billie shook her head. "He's too young. All we can do is treat the pain."

Suspicion twinged like the ache from a sore tooth. Could *Billie* be behind the pharmacy thefts?

You got a problem with personal use, Tom Dietz had said. *Somebody with access.*

Nell's chest felt tight. Not Billie. If Billie were using, Nell would know. There were signs, symptoms… But what if Billie were taking the drugs for her nephew?

She didn't have the code to the narcotics closet. But she had handled the pharmacy keys. She could have seen Nell enter the code.

Nell couldn't believe the other nurse would violate everything—the law, her training and their friendship—to steal from the clinic. She didn't want to believe it. Since her mother died and her husband dumped her, her clinic co-workers were the only family she had.

But then, two years ago, Nell hadn't wanted to believe Richard could betray her, either, and her willful blindness then had almost destroyed them both.

She forced herself to breathe. "So, have you… Is Trevor getting enough medication?"

Billie shrugged. "What's enough? He's trying

those pain management techniques, the imaging and stuff, but it's hard. He's only nine years old.''

''His mother could help him,'' Nell said, amazed at how natural she sounded.

''Crystal has to work. The only one who can keep an eye on Trev during the day is that lameass boyfriend of hers.''

That wasn't good. Complications could develop rapidly with sickle cell. Patients' families had to know what symptoms to watch for and how to respond to them.

Maybe it was in Trevor's best interests if Nell took a look at his chart.

And maybe Nell was a lying, scheming, mistrustful bitch who wanted to check the boy's pain treatment plan to see if his aunt Billie had any motive to steal.

''I could take a look at his chart,'' Nell said. ''Maybe offer a second opinion.''

''Sure,'' Billie said slowly. ''That would be... great.''

Yeah, great, Nell thought as Billie disappeared into Exam Four with her plastic-wrapped syringes. She stared blindly at the photo of mother and child taped to the wall. She was already in trouble with the state Nursing Board. The last thing she needed was to discover a nurse she'd hired, a friend, was skimming Schedule Two drugs from the pharmacy.

Not to mention that if Fletcher discovered her reviewing the boy's chart, he'd have every right to complain she was overstepping her authority with his patient.

''You know they named her after you,'' Joe said behind her. ''The baby. They named her Elena.''

Nell's heart thumped. She turned.

And there he was, standing in the aisle in front of the nurses' station with his thumbs in his belt loops and a gleam in his eye, lean and tough and hot. She was so glad to see him it made her cross.

"What are you doing here?"

"I came to see you," he said, just the way she'd hoped he would four days ago when he brought Laila to the clinic to have her baby.

Four days ago.

Four days.

Without a phone call.

She lifted her chin. "Why? You finished your story."

Joe nodded, still with that unsettling glint in his eyes. "That's why."

"I don't understand," Nell said.

"You mean you don't remember." He took a step closer, taking up more space and more oxygen than a man his size had a right to. "I told you that first night at Flynn's. Once I file the story, I don't have any rules against taking you to bed."

Chapter 6

Nell was wound as tight as an Ace bandage, nearly breathless with distress. She couldn't deal with Joe Reilly's particular brand of shark charm right now.

She eyed him warily. "Don't tell me that line has ever actually worked on anyone."

Joe grinned at her, hot and male and so irresistibly sexy she wanted to slug him. "There's always a first time."

Oh, great. Her world was falling apart, and he was doing Sexual Banter. Banter was interesting, banter was fine when you had the energy, but just this once Nell wished she could fall for a guy who expressed himself by grunting comfort or buying flowers. Roses would be nice. Red ones. Something predictable, something she could count on.

She pulled herself together. "This isn't a first time for either one of us. And there's no way I'd have sex with you as a reward for some four-inch sidebar in the paper.''

Joe looked wounded. ''I didn't think size mattered to you.''

Lucy Morales dropped her pen and bent to pick it up, her shoulders shaking with laughter.

Nell was too tired for this. But she rallied like the fighter she was. ''It's not the size, Reilly. It's what you do with it.''

His eyes sharpened. His face sobered. ''You didn't like the story?''

Tired or not, worried or not, she couldn't let him think for one minute that his words hadn't touched her.

''I loved it,'' she said honestly. ''You made me cry.''

He continued to study her, his hands in his pockets. ''Not exactly the reaction I was hoping for. But thanks.''

His continued attention made her uncomfortable. ''What did your editor think?''

''He was okay with it.''

Nell sighed. The clinic was as crowded as Wrigley Field on an August afternoon. The waiting room was full, the exam rooms were loaded, she had a probable respiratory infection on deck and a return patient with diabetes in the dugout. Someone close to her was stealing drugs from the clinic pharmacy, and she'd just pretended concern for a sick child so she could pin a motive on her best friend.

She was as exhausted and empty as a used syringe. The last thing she needed was to take on responsibility for Joe or his story or his future.

But she couldn't let it go.

"Just okay?"

"More than okay," Joe admitted. "Health care's hot right now. He wants me to do some kind of series on medical insurance."

"That's exciting," Nell said. Except you'd never guess it from Joe's stolid face. "Isn't it?"

"Yeah. Exciting. You give me the statistics, I'll give you a story."

That was what she wanted, wasn't it? A well-researched feature to drum up donations. But…

"It's not about statistics," Nell objected. "My patients aren't numbers. They're people. That's your story."

"Real life-or-death stuff." His tone was dry.

Nell looked him in the eye. He was so not getting away with that. "It is for them."

"Right. Everybody has a story. That doesn't make it news."

"But…" She couldn't reconcile this Joe with the man who had coached Laila through her daughter's birth, the reporter who had conveyed her story with such insight and compassion. "You wrote about the Massouds."

"And it ended up on the front page of the Life section."

She was genuinely bewildered. "What's the matter with that?"

"It would never run on page one. The rule of journalism is, if it bleeds, it leads."

His attitude was pissing her off. "And that's important to you? Being on page one."

His blue eyes blazed. And then his heavy lids dropped over them, and he shrugged. "Yeah. At least it used to be."

"Then I guess you'll have to do a good enough job with this series to compel your editor to run your story on the front page. Maybe I can find someone who's bleeding for you."

"Damn it, Dolan." Joe sounded more weary than angry. "Don't you ever give up?"

His question shook loose a swarm of memories, already buzzing and crawling in the wake of the pharmacy thefts. Memories of being a teenager coming home from school to deal with the morning's dishes and the evening's meal and her mother's increasingly fragile health. Memories of being a young wife coming home from a full day of work to a week's worth of laundry and a month's worth of bills and an increasingly demanding and critical husband.

"Sometimes I want to." The confession popped out. She could tell her admission surprised him. Well, it surprised her, too. She raised her chin. "But it's not usually an option."

She was like the grandfather clock in his parents' dining room, Joe thought. That pale, beautiful face hid the ticking brain inside and a bundle of nerves wound tight.

He felt an almost irresistible urge to comfort her and shoved his hands deep in his pockets so he wouldn't do something stupid with them, like pat her on the back or pull her close. He didn't want to comfort her.

In fact, he thought, trying to work up some indignation with the idea, Nell Dolan was one of the most uncomfortable people he had ever known. Talking with her was like walking on a leg that had fallen asleep. One minute he was nice and numb, not feeling much of anything, and then she came along pushing and prodding, forcing him to life, making him prickle with returning sensation.

The woman was a pain.

But Joe had to admit he was kind of relieved to know he had some feeling left after all.

"You want a story?" he asked. "I'll write a story that will impress your pants off. But you have to co-operate."

The chin went up another notch. "By taking off my pants?"

Joe grinned. "That would be a bonus," he said. "Actually, I was angling for access to some information, maybe the chance to talk with some of your volunteers."

She hesitated. "I can give you names. I can't guar-antee they'll talk to you."

He shrugged. "It's a place to start."

And he wanted a start, he realized. His career might be at a standstill, his ankle was a dead end, but he wanted another start with her.

"And I want you to clear discussions with my staff through me," Nell added.

Joe raised his eyebrows. "You protecting some-body, Dolan?"

She went white, then red. "From you? Now, why would I feel the need to do that?" -

"That's what I'd like to know," Joe said frankly.

But if he thought he could tempt her into confiding in him, he'd underestimated her.

Nell shuffled through the folders on the counter with the authority of a Las Vegas dealer before she selected one and attempted to step around him. "Maybe you make me nervous."

He didn't budge. "I know how to change that."

"You're leaving?"

He grinned down at her, enjoying the frosty note in her voice and the smell of her hair. "Not a chance. Have dinner with me."

She clutched her folder tighter. "Like that worked before."

"This time will be different," he promised rashly.

Would it? Why did he want it to be?

Because she was different, he thought. Or he was.

"Different, how?"

"Trust me."

Her eyes searched his. "I can't," she said finally. "I have plans tonight."

He wasn't exactly in a position to object to her seeing other guys. That didn't mean he had to like it. "I'll make you a deal. I'll agree to check with you before I interview anyone if you agree to dinner."

"When? I told you, I have—"

"Sunday," Joe said desperately. This was such a bad idea. Except his mother would be thrilled. But maybe the visit would get her off his back. Maybe he could kill two birds with one stone, lull Nell to the point that he could talk her into bed and convince his family he was finding his feet again.

His family.

His mother would exclaim. His father would sit silently and watch her over his Guinness. And his brothers... His brothers would have a field day if he showed up for Sunday dinner with blond, Irish Catholic nurse Nell Dolan by his side.

Nell's brow pleated. "I guess Sunday would work. What time?"

He would just have to kill them, Joe thought, resigned.

"Five o'clock," he said. "I'll pick you up."

He was feeling pretty good as he walked away.

So of course whatever gods had it in for him only let him get halfway to the door before he heard Nell ask, "Are you all right?"

Hell.

Joe pivoted, careful to keep his weight on his right leg. "Yeah, fine."

"Because you're limping again."

"I overdid it the other day."

And hadn't been able to walk without crutches for almost two. Despite the stirrup brace he'd strapped on before leaving the house this morning, his bones ground together. He could almost feel the screws working loose as his ankle became more and more deformed.

"Guess I should ice my ankle when I get home," he said easily.

"Do you have something you can take for it?" Nell asked.

Joe felt something coiling in his gut like panic. Or hunger. It couldn't be that easy. He couldn't resist... "You mean, like painkillers?"

Nell frowned. "Actually, I was thinking of an anti-inflammatory."

Joe's gut relaxed. He exhaled. "Yeah. Yeah, I've got something. Thanks."

He said goodbye and left. Despite his slow pace, he was sweating as if he'd run a mile.

Nell ate her yogurt at her desk while she read up on bimalleolar injury and deltoid ligament rupture.

She saw a lot of ankle injuries at the clinic. Basketball players, mostly, from the playgrounds and streets. Skateboarders. Tenants who slipped on their fire escapes, the elderly who tripped in their kitchens. Ninety percent of the injuries were sprains. Very few were actual fractures.

But even the fractures generally healed in four to six weeks. After eight, referral to an orthopedist was mandatory.

She jabbed her plastic spoon into the carton. Joe wasn't her patient. He didn't want to be.

Which was fine by Nell. She hadn't been able to cure her own mother. She hadn't been able to help her own husband. She definitely wasn't seeking responsibility for another wounded male. She could handle a stable type A fracture, but she wasn't even qualified to treat a complex orthopedic injury.

But Joe's limp nagged at her. If the shape and anatomy of an ankle were not accurately restored after a trauma, the patient suffered chronic pain, early arthritis, even deformity. How long had Joe been living with the pain in his left ankle?

"Nell?" Melody slid around the filing cabinets, blinking inoffensively. Her eyelids today were bright green. "You have a patient on line two. Judith Lawrence? She's having some kind of problem getting a prescription filled."

Nell abandoned the problem of Joe's ankle while she pulled up the Lawrence medical file. Judith Lawrence, thirty-eight, white female, recurrent kidney stones. Nell had seen her on Wednesday for cramps in her side and lower abdomen. She'd treated her for the pain and sent her home with instructions to drink two to three quarts of water a day until the stone passed.

Nell punched line two. "Hi, Judith. This is Eleanor Dolan. How are you doing?"

She listened as Judith, an experienced patient, ran down her list of symptoms. No fever or chills that would indicate an infection. No blood in her urine. Just the pain.

"I thought I was managing," Judith said, almost apologetically. "But I felt so much worse last night my husband went to get that prescription for Tylenol 3 you gave me, and the pharmacist wouldn't fill it."

Nell made a note. "Did he tell you why?"

"He said the insurance company refused to authorize payment."

A premonition of trouble fluttered, soft as moth wings in the dark. Nell brushed it away.

"Do you have drug insurance?"

"I have an independent co-payment plan," Judith said. "But, honestly, if it's this much trouble, we can't afford to keep it."

"All right, I'll call the pharmacist," Nell said. "I can authorize a new prescription if it's necessary. You just rest and drink plenty of fluids and get back to me if you experience any problems."

Judith Lawrence was a regular patient with a legitimate medical complaint, Nell assured herself as she waited on hold to speak with the pharmacist. Not a doctor-shopper. Not a drug abuser.

But when the pharmacist came on the line, he was adamant that a prescription had already been filled almost a week ago, before Judith came in complaining of pain. Fourteen days' supply, well in excess of the two or three days' required to get her patient through the usual discomfort of passing a stone. The insurance company was refusing payment until the term of the original dosage expired.

Nell's heart hammered.

"Do you remember who picked up the prescription?" she asked.

The pharmacist sighed. "No, I don't. But you wrote it."

Nell felt cold. She hadn't. She wouldn't. She never prescribed narcotics without seeing the patient. She knew better.

She thanked the pharmacist and hung up, her hand shaking, feeling as though she'd slid down a long, dark tunnel into an old, recurring nightmare. A bad one. There was that same sense of suffocating terror, of breathless futility, of things waiting to catch her out. To trip her up. To devour her.

Just to be sure, Nell combed through Judith's file and her own appointment record in case there had been a meeting, a phone call, a contact she'd forgotten.

Nothing.

Which meant someone, somehow, must have copied or forged an old prescription. Judith? Or someone with access to Nell's prescription pad and the clinic's patient list?

Blood rushed in her ears. Nell resisted the urge to lower her head between her knees. She was not going to faint. She was not going to panic. Last time she'd panicked, and she'd paid.

This time she was going to be calm and in control and follow protocol exactly. She hadn't done anything wrong. All she had to do was call the police. She would be very honest, very open, and…

And pray to God, Joe Reilly didn't find out and use her troubles to catapult himself back onto the front page of the *Examiner*.

It was Friday, and Joe's youngest brother had apparently pulled the job of baby-sitting Joe for the night. Or else he wanted to watch the game without their mother scolding him about wet rings on the coffee table.

"Saw your drug dealer yesterday," Mike remarked as he reached for the pretzels.

Joe froze with his hand wrapped around a can of Coke and his gaze fixed on the TV. The Bulls were down by seven in the second quarter. When he trusted himself to speak, he growled, "What are you talking about?"

His brother leaned out of his seat. "No, no, no, don't let Odom have the ball! Jesus, Mary and Joseph, they're throwing this game away."

Odom passed to Darius Miles, who went for the layup. Down by nine to the Clippers.

Joe rotated the sweating can in his hands. "Mike. What the hell are you talking about?"

"I'm talking about their lousy passing." Mike stuffed another pretzel in his mouth and then grinned through the crumbs. "Oh. Before. The blonde. The nurse? We got called to her clinic because she was writing bad prescriptions."

Joe watched as possession went to the Bulls. His gut churned. His mind spun. Nell, clear-eyed, conscientious, compassionate Nell, involved in prescription fraud?

"Is this some kind of joke?" he demanded. "April Fools'?"

"That was yesterday," Mike protested, all inno-cence.

Joe narrowed his eyes.

"Okay." Mike held up both hands, palms out. "So I tweaked the story to get a rise out of you. But we did get a call."

Joe was still dizzy. Lack of oxygen. He hadn't breathed since his idiot brother dropped his bomb-shell. "Who called you?"

"She did. Dolan."

Anger flared, catching Joe off guard. "Then you can't honestly think—"

"That your girlfriend's involved in drug fraud? I've got an open mind."

"What about your partner, Dietz? Does he have an open mind, too?"

"Tom's reserving judgment."

"But he's seen her. Talked with her."

"We both talked with her. She's saying somebody either photocopied an old prescription or stole her prescription pad and forged her signature."

"That happens, doesn't it?"

"Happens all the time," Mike agreed. "But when we collected the scrip from the pharmacy, it sure looked legit to me. Standard abbreviations. Real ink. Bad handwriting."

"Signature?" Joe asked, trying to sound like he was just after the truth, Joe Objective Journalist in-stead of Joe the Schmuck Who Cared.

"Looked like a match. But then, I've seen you sign notes from school so the teacher never knew they weren't from Mom. So a forger could have copied her signature."

"Are you—" Joe's throat constricted. Stupid. This

was no big deal. Police blotter stuff. Only he doubted Nell would be able to see it that way. "Are you going to charge her?"

"Not yet. Sergeant'll probably put a detective on it, though."

"Is it that serious? One patient altering one prescription?"

"If that's all it is. But we have to look for a pattern of abuse. Word is, there's been an increase in the number of prescription drugs hitting the street."

That was bad. But Joe's brain automatically kept on asking questions, testing theories, going after the facts.

"How recent an increase?" he asked.

"Recent," Mike repeated, which meant he either didn't know or couldn't say. "Beats me why the dealers want to move in on Tylenol when they've got the corner on the crack market already, but that's what's got the brass excited."

"Prescription drugs have better potency, consistency and purity than most street drugs," Joe said. "Which gives them a higher resale value, too."

"Nice to know." Mike watched as Jay Williams drove to the basket and scored. He turned his head, his eyes cool and flat, so that for a second he didn't look like Joe's baby brother at all. He looked like a cop. "How do you know?"

Joe's hand tightened on his soda can.

"Research," he said.

Experience.

But some things he couldn't say. Not to his brother. *Admit to God, to myself and to another human being the exact nature of my wrongs,* fine. But not his brothers. Not his parents. God spare them all that.

"Some story you were doing, huh?" asked Mike. Next he was going to ask to read it.

"Background stuff," Joe said. "You never know what you can use somewhere down the road."

"Yeah." Mike grabbed another pretzel. "Maybe you'll write the big story—Nurse Dolan Does Drug Diversion on the North Side."

Joe's jaw set. "You don't really think she's done anything wrong."

Mike shrugged. "I don't know. I like her. But Tom says in a lot of cases like this, the practitioner is working with the pharmacy. Maybe she uses, too. Or maybe she gets a kickback from the pharmacy."

"Except in this case, the pharmacy didn't fill the prescription."

"So that lets them off the hook. Not the blonde."

Temper licked through Joe at his brother's casual tone. At his careless appraisal of someone as good, as principled, as dedicated as Nell. "Her name is Nell."

"I know her—" Mike paused with a pretzel halfway to his mouth. "Hell. Are you sweet on her?"

"What is this, high school? No, I'm not sweet on her. I just think you should have some respect for the work she does, that's all."

Mike's face turned red. The curse of the fair-skinned Irish. "I respect her. But being a nurse doesn't mean she can't be a druggie. In fact, more medical professionals become addicts because they have access to drugs."

"Right. And more cops shoot their wives because they have access to guns."

Mike put down his pretzel. He picked up his beer

and took a long, slow swallow while Joe cursed himself silently. He shouldn't have gone there.

Mike wiped his mouth with the back of his hand. "You forgot brothers. We shoot our brothers, too."

He was forgiven. Cautiously, Joe relaxed. "Should I duck under the couch?"

"Naw. But you could bring me another beer."

"You got it." Joe levered himself to his feet, relieved that things were back to normal. Mike never could hold a grudge.

But as he hobbled to the kitchen, his brother called, "Wait till I tell Mom you're sweet on the nurse."

Chapter 7

She couldn't go through with it, Nell decided, staring at her reflection in the bathroom mirror. Her reflection stared back, eyes dark with worry, mouth tight with strain.

She didn't look like a woman getting ready for a date. She looked like a woman preparing for an audit from the IRS.

Nell resisted the urge to drag her hands through her hair and undo the careful curl achieved with her styling brush and blow-dryer. No wonder she never went out. Oh, she'd snuck out a few times in high school, experimenting with rebellion, torn by guilt. But for most of her adult life, she had been too stressed-out, too overcommitted, for the time-consuming rituals of Boy Dates Girl.

And that was before she became a suspect in an ongoing drug investigation.

At least she didn't have to worry Joe was going to

dissect Billie in his newspaper. Yesterday, Nell had reviewed nine-year-old Trevor Parker's chart. Billie's nephew was receiving more than adequate levels of pain medication. James Fletcher's treatment plan might not be alleviating all the boy's symptoms, but it certainly didn't provide a motive for his aunt to steal drugs.

So Billie was out. That only left Ed Johnson, Melody King, Lucy Morales and several dozen volunteer nurses and physicians as suspects. All her friends, her surrogate family.

And Nell herself.

She scowled and dabbed blusher on her face. The makeup stood out like fever spots against her pale skin. What was she thinking? Any relationship now would be a distraction.

A relationship with Joe Reilly would be a disaster.

She needed support, stability, control. All the things her lonely, workaholic childhood lacked. All the things her empty, crumbling marriage hadn't been able to provide. She was out of her mind to think she could find them with a burned-out, cynical reporter in need of healing whose brother was one of the cops trying to tie her to prescription fraud.

She should never have agreed to have dinner with him. She should have called to cancel. She would have called, except she didn't have Joe's home number, and the newspaper switchboard was probably closed on weekends.

Nell met the eyes of the woman in the mirror. *Liar.* She could have reached Joe if she wanted to. Obviously, she didn't want to.

No, what she wanted was to forget all the reasons she couldn't behave like an ordinary thirty-year-old woman with a normal sex drive. Forget her troubles and responsibilities. Forget the Angel of Ark Street. For once, she wanted to be selfish and have a good time.

She had a sudden vision of Joe, of his weary eyes and knowing grin, his surgeon's hands and lean, tough body. He would be a good time, she thought wistfully.

Being good hadn't earned Nell her mother's attention or secured her husband's love. Maybe it was time to see what being bad could do for her.

The buzzer rasped. Nell felt a purely feminine flutter as she pressed the button that released the security door downstairs. She stood in the hallway, her hands clasped nervously together, waiting for Joe's knock.

A quick tattoo announced his arrival. Taking a deep breath, Nell opened the door.

She had dressed with care in khaki slacks and a pink silk twinset, a leftover from her doctor's wife wardrobe.

Joe wore jeans and work boots and a deep blue shirt that matched his eyes. He looked so good her stomach contracted with lust. And then twisted with something else. Surprise. Delight. Longing.

He'd brought her flowers.

Not roses. Daffodils, tiny ones, the kind you could buy at the grocery store on the corner. Their bright gold trumpets and green spears rose bravely from a purple plastic pot.

"Here." He thrust them at her.

"Thank you." Not good enough. She tried again. "They're beautiful." The gesture was so unexpected, so unlike what she thought she knew of him, she was at a loss for words. Unable to help herself, she lifted the flowers to her face. The bright blooms had little scent, but their touch on her cheek was cool and gentle. "You didn't have to bring me flowers."

"Yeah, I did." Joe sounded grim. "You don't know where I'm taking you for dinner yet."

Amused, she smiled. "Bribes, Reilly?"

"I was thinking more along the line of incentives. These are for you." He took the pot from her and set it on the hall table, already overflowing with bills and circulars. "And this—"

He cupped her shoulders. His hands were hard and warm. "This is for me."

He tugged her against him, slid one hand into her hair and pulled her mouth to his.

Shock held her still.

He wasn't persuasive or coaxing this time. He was urgent. Rough. Nipping at her lower lip, he plundered her mouth.

Her heart slammed against her ribs. Sensation crashed through her. He tasted like mint and smelled of tobacco and kissed as if he had something to prove. To her? Or to himself? But the thought dissolved as his tongue demanded her response and her mind turned to mush. Power, pleasure, desire swamped her body and rushed through her blood. It was wonderful.

It was insane.

Her arms were trapped between them. She wanted to touch, to feel him, and struggled to free her hands. He shifted just enough to allow her to slide her palms around his lean waist and up his muscled back. Amazing. They fit together, breast to chest, belly to belly, heat to heat. The hard ridge of his erection rode between her thighs. She rubbed against him like a cat, and he grunted and backed her into the wall.

Her head hit plaster. Her teeth bumped his lip.

He lifted his mouth. "Ouch. Are you—"

Impatient, she drew him back. "More."

He grinned, but she saw with satisfaction that he was breathing as hard as she was. And he gave her more, deep, wet, hungry kisses that fed and left her wanting at the same time. His arms were solid around her, his hot, insistent mouth making her mind a blissful blank.

Which was wonderful, Nell told herself, because as long as her brain was fogged with sex, as long as she was warming herself with his heat and breathing his breath and pulsing with his rhythm, she didn't have to think about... She wasn't going to think about...

His hand closed over her breast, firm, possessive, and whatever it was she wasn't thinking slid farther below the surface. Gratefully, she sucked in her breath; released it on a moan.

But when his hand slid under the hem of her sweater, his warm fingers brushing bare skin, a glint of sanity slipped through her absorption like the crack of light beneath a door.

One part of her accepted where this was going. The inevitability of it pounded in her chest. His arousal pressed purposefully against the seam of her thighs. They were both adults. They'd known each other... Okay, a week wasn't all that long. But he wanted her, and she wanted the forgetfulness she was pretty sure he could give her. Maybe it wasn't wise, maybe it wasn't romantic, but she was going to make love with Joe Reilly.

But not standing up in the hall. She wanted, needed, more romance than that.

She eased her mouth away from his with tiny, tasting kisses. "Joe."

"Yes." His voice was hoarse. His forehead was damp. "Whatever it is, yes."

She flushed with pleasure. "Do you…"

She bit her lip, that sense of inevitability, the it-had-to-be-you-and-now feeling, fading a bit. It was so much easier to be swept away than to make a choice. A demand.

"Do you want to have dinner first?" she asked, which wasn't what she'd started to say at all.

Joe smiled at her with those brooding blue eyes, making her pulse hitch. Maybe he was going to sweep her away after all, she thought hopefully.

"No, I don't want—" His face went utterly blank. "Oh God. Dinner."

Alarmed, Nell asked, "What's wrong?"

His hand slid from under her sweater. "What time is it?"

Trying not to feel insulted, Nell looked at her watch. "Five-twenty. Why? Do we have reservations?"

"I wish. We could cancel reservations."

But if they weren't going out…

"Where are you taking me?" Nell asked.

Not to bed, obviously. Her chest burned with disappointment.

"Home," Joe said.

"You're cooking?" Maybe he had a roast in the oven.

"No. My mother is." For once, Joe's smile was more sheepish than sharklike. "I'm taking you home with me for Sunday dinner."

* * *

He must have been out of his mind, Joe thought. He watched through the kitchen door as Nell chopped—what was it, carrots?—with his mother.

They could have stayed at her apartment. He could have had her in her bed, all the clean lines and soft curves of her, her fair skin stained with color, her clear eyes dark with desire. The thought of her, of what he was missing, buzzed in his blood and put an edge on his mood.

"Sulking," Will observed, not unsympathetically, as he sprawled on the couch. "Because Mom poached his date. You should have known what would happen when you invited her, paperboy."

Mike looked over from setting the table. The good china, Joe noted, and the lace tablecloth. He was in such deep trouble here.

"Why did you invite her, anyway?" asked his brother the cop.

Will raised his eyebrows. "What are you, blind? She's hot. I'd have invited her myself, except then Mom would be grilling her about *my* sex life over the salad."

Joe wished he and his brothers were fifteen, thirteen and ten again, so he could pound them into silence.

But their father spoke from his chair by the window. "She seems like a nice girl. And your mother likes having somebody to keep her company in the kitchen."

"I keep her company," Mike said.

"You're twenty-five-years old and still living in the basement," said Ted Reilly. "Your mother gets enough of your company."

Will snorted with laughter.

Mike threw the bread basket at his head. Will grabbed it out of the air, sending rolls bouncing on the pillows of the couch.

"Do I need to come out there?" Mary called from the kitchen.

"No, ma'am," her sons chorused.

Will picked up the rolls and launched them one by one at Mike, who brushed them off and dropped them on the table.

They might as well be fifteen, thirteen and ten again, Joe thought. Except for him. He didn't play anymore. They didn't expect him to. He bent to pick up the basket.

"So, I hear your young lady is a nurse," Ted said.

Joe straightened cautiously. "That's right."

"You meet her at the hospital?"

"No, a clinic. I'm writing a story about her clinic. I'm not her patient."

"Ah," Ted said, and took a pull of his beer.

Joe was a reporter. He knew the tricks. So he didn't fall for the old man's say-anything-to-fill-the-silence ploy.

He glanced toward the kitchen where the two women had their heads together over the roasting pan. None of her menfolk—not her oldest son the reporter or her youngest son the cop—was a match for Mary Reilly when it came to getting information. So he could still be in trouble.

As he watched, Nell looked up from the stove and met his gaze. The rueful appeal in her eyes tore into his chest like a bullet.

His breath stopped. Trouble? Oh, yeah.

Setting the bread basket on the table, he limped to her rescue.

* * *

Mary Reilly was five foot two and fifty-three, with an explosion of charcoal curls, a quick smile and deft hands. Nell liked her immediately.

"I'm not much of a cook," she apologized, sweeping her misshapen carrot slices into a wooden bowl.

"Plenty of time to learn," Mary said. "Does your mother cook?"

After Nell's father left them, Alice Dolan had struggled to hold two jobs, manning a cash register in the daytime and cleaning offices at night. As far back as Nell could remember, dinner had consisted of whatever she could pour from a can or heat in the microwave.

"My mother died eight years ago," Nell said.

Mary made a soft, sympathetic sound. "Well, the salad looks lovely," she said. "And as long as we're putting dinner on the table, that lot out there can eat it and be grateful."

"Don't you make them help?" Nell asked.

"I make them offer," Mary said. "Truth is, I like to cook, and they get in the way."

She proved her point by opening the oven door and forcing Nell back against the counter. Grabbing pot holders, Mary wrestled her roasting pan to the top of the stove. Fabulous smells assaulted the air, rosemary, beef and bacon. Nell's mouth watered.

Mary transferred the roast to a carving board and started to make gravy in the pan.

"You shouldn't have gone to so much trouble," Nell said.

Mary grinned, looking for a moment startlingly like Joe. "This isn't trouble. I was going to make codfish with garlic sauce, but I didn't want to give Ted heartburn.'' She whisked beef broth into the pan, shaking her head. ''Irish men.''

Unable to resist the smells, Nell took a step closer to the stove. ''You're not Irish?''

''Half Irish. My mother was a Cifelli. What about you?''

Nell smiled. ''With a name like Dolan? I'm Irish.''

''I thought that might be your husband's name.'' Mary ground black pepper over the bubbling gravy. Tasted. ''One of the boys mentioned you'd been married.''

She was like a surgeon, probing and digging until she'd extracted something. Nell looked around rather wildly for reinforcements and caught Joe's cynical eye. No help there.

''My husband's name was Burdett,'' she said.

Mary sniffed and poured the gravy into a large white boat. ''Sounds like an Orangeman.''

''I don't know what he was, actually.''

A liar. A junkie.

''Protestant, though.'' Mary spooned roasted potatoes around the beef.

''Yes.'' What did it matter?

''That's all right, then,'' Mary said with satisfaction.

''Ma, in her infinitely tactful way, is trying to find out if you were ever married in the church,'' Joe drawled, strolling into the kitchen.

Nell was grateful for the interruption. But she still didn't get it. ''No, the Drake Hotel. Why?''

''Because this way we're still eligible for a large Catholic wedding.''

Nell's jaw dropped.

Joe grinned and pressed a firm, brief kiss on her

open mouth. "Don't panic. Since we're only going to indulge in a torrid, temporary affair, it doesn't matter to me either way."

Mary clicked her tongue. "Stop trying to shock the girl, Joseph, and take out the roast."

"I was trying to shock *you*," he complained, but he carried the carving board through the door to the table.

"Don't mind him," Mary said, handing the gravy boat to Nell. "Or me, either. We're all too free in speaking our minds."

Nell murmured something and fled in the direction of the dining room.

She didn't have any reason to feel nervous or embarrassed. *She* wasn't the one asking intensely personal questions or making outrageous personal announcements.

Her hand shook slightly as she set down the gravy boat. Nell bit her lip. She was not going to spill on her hostess's lovely old lace tablecloth.

A large Catholic wedding?

Or *a torrid, temporary affair?*

She got hot just thinking about it. Hot and terrified. She'd made a mess of her marriage. And the possibility of conducting a torrid affair under the curious eyes of Joe's family... No, she couldn't do that, either.

To her relief, the conversation over dinner stayed general. Everyone seemed to talk, tease and eat with their mouths full. The Reillys passed bowls, heaped plates and argued amiably about video games and precinct politics, this uncle's new car and that neighbor's lawn, the Bulls' dismal chances in the play-offs and the start of the Cubs' season. It was chaotic, it was comfortable, it was intimate and alien at the same time.

Dinner with her mother had been a mostly silent affair, punctuated by celebrity news and canned laughter from the TV. Richard had seldom been home for dinner during their marriage; even when he wasn't working, he preferred to go out or claimed he was too exhausted to talk. To her. To keep the peace, to preserve her marriage, Nell had accepted the painful truth: she simply wasn't very interesting to her husband. And so she had settled for the gossipy camaraderie of her co-workers, the loyalties created by late hours and bad coffee, the bonds forged by the hectic pace and shared purpose of the work lane.

The ties between the Reillys were different, but Nell felt their pull all around the table. These were ties of affection. Of habit and history. Of love and blood.

Cynical Reilly the reporter was a family man. The thought made Nell smile. Made her yearn.

And yet, sitting at the noisy table, she sensed a wall around him, a barrier that laughter and affection could not breach. It was subtle, hinted in a look, heard in a deflected question.

Will got up to clear the table, balancing two plates in each large hand.

"I'll wash, you dry," Mike volunteered, tipping his chair back from the table.

Nell laid her knife and fork across her plate. Maybe, she mused, she recognized Joe's essential isolation because she was an outsider herself.

"Hell, no," Will growled. "I'm clearing. Joe can dry."

"Drying's for fairies," Joe said. "I'll wash. Mike can dry."

Bemused, Nell watched a general scuffle develop in the kitchen door, with lots of shoulder bumping and elbow jabs.

Isolated? Right. And maybe she was imagining things.

Mary flinched, her attention on the doorway. Her sons jostled through, and her shoulders slowly relaxed.

"Sorry about that." Mary met Nell's gaze, her eyes rueful. It wasn't clear if she was apologizing for the scuffle or her own reaction to it. "I worry about Joe's ankle."

She shouldn't ask.

She wouldn't ask.

He wasn't her patient, it was none of her business...

"What's wrong with his ankle, exactly?"

"Well, he broke it," Mary said.

"Yes, he told me."

Or rather, his brother did.

"I don't know how bad the initial fracture was, but he didn't treat it properly while he was over there," Mary confided. "He said he got some kind of boot cast put on it, but he didn't rest it properly. I know he kept working. Eventually he, well, he just collapsed."

Even though Nell figured Joe's complications were probably the result of his own stubbornness, her heart squeezed at the thought of him hurting and helpless and miles from home.

"So, what happened?" she asked.

"The paper brought him home," his father said gruffly.

Mary covered her husband's hand with her own. The gesture spoke volumes about Joe's condition, Nell thought. And his parents' relationship.

"Joe had surgery to repair the fracture alignment," Mary said. "A screw and plate fixation, the doctor called it."

Nell nodded.

"But it didn't heal correctly," Mary continued. "He needs to have the surgery redone. A complete reconstruction of the ankle, the doctor said."

"Won't do it," Ted said. "Damn fool."

His gaze shifted. His broad face flushed.

Oh, no, Nell thought, and turned her head.

Joe stood in the kitchen doorway. His mouth was grim. His eyes were blazing blue. Clearly, he'd overheard at least part of their conversation. Equally obviously, he was furious.

Nell's stomach sank.

"The dishes are done," he said coldly. "When you all are finished discussing my personal medical history, I'm ready to go."

Chapter 8

It was his own damn fault, Joe accepted grimly, for being stupid enough to break his own rules.

It was Nell's fault, for being compassionate and caring and worming her way into his parents' confidence.

He stalked up the stairs behind her to her third-floor apartment, burning with anger at her intrusion and eaten with fear at what she could have discovered.

He had to protect himself.

Joe leaned his weight on the banister, doing his best to ignore the grinding in his ankle. Trying not to notice the sway and flex of Nell's butt half a flight above him.

Before he hauled her off to bed, they were going to get some things straight. Right now.

Nell reached the landing and stood with her keys

in her hand. Waiting for him. The realization that she needed to wait only pissed him off more.

Joe pulled himself up the last two steps and leaned an arm against the wall above her head, supporting himself, trapping her.

He put his face down into her face and said with soft menace, "If I need your help, I'll tell you. In the meantime, keep your nose out of my business."

Of course, Nell being Nell was not impressed. "That tone doesn't exactly work for me, Reilly."

"You know what doesn't work for me? You talking to my parents about my ankle. If you were that curious, you could have asked me."

"And would you have told me anything?"

He wasn't in the mood to be managed or reasoned with. "That's not the point."

"That's precisely the point. Two people can't form a relationship without sharing some details of their personal lives."

"Some details," he repeated with heavy sarcasm. "How much sharing are you willing to do, Mrs. Burdett?"

The color drained from her face. Her eyes were bright and angry. Joe felt like a jerk. But in some twisted way he was relieved to know he could get to her the way she got to him.

"You knew I'd been married before," she said.

"And you knew I'd busted my ankle. That doesn't entitle you to all the gory details."

"I was trying to help."

"Well, don't."

He didn't want her help.

He didn't want her pity.

He wanted her admiring. And preferably naked. And soon.

"Fine." Nell ducked under his arm and unlocked her door with jerky movements.

"Where are you going?"

"I believe this discussion is over."

Thank God. Now that she understood his limits, maybe they could finally get somewhere.

He'd been on edge all evening, his body fired and his imagination fueled by the memory of her warm and soft and pressed against the wall. Watching her smiling and relaxed with his family, he'd burned for her. He liked her, damn it. That didn't mean he had to spill his guts to her until they both floundered in the slippery mess.

He flattened his hand against the door to hold it open.

Nell turned her head, her hair brushing his cheek. "What are you doing?"

Joe narrowed his eyes in surprise. "I'm coming in with you."

"No, you're not. I am not having sex with a man who puts restrictions up front on our relationship."

Frustration made him blunt. "It didn't bother you before dinner that there were restrictions on our relationship."

Her mouth opened. Closed. A pink flush moved up her pale cheeks. God, she was pretty.

Gotcha, Joe thought smugly.

But he was wrong.

"You were the one who took me to meet your family," Nell pointed out.

Cool, he thought, admiring and resentful. How could she be so cool?

He stuck his thumbs through his belt loops. "So?"

"So it bothers me now." She slipped inside.

He was losing her.

"Why don't we both sleep on it?" he suggested. "You can kick me out in the morning if you change your mind."

"Thank you for the very attractive offer. But no."

She leaned on the door to shut it. He resisted the urge to stick his foot over the threshold like a damn salesman.

"No good-night kiss?" he taunted.

The door jerked open again.

Nell stood framed in the opening. "Okay."

Before he could think, before he could react, she stepped up to him and twined her arms around his neck.

She planted one right on his mouth. Full. Hot. Wet. Deep. She curled his toes. She fried his brain. And then, when his fingers flexed on her back and his stunned mind struggled to catch up with his amazed and grateful body, she dropped her arms and stepped back into her apartment.

"Sleep on that," she said, and shut the door in his face.

No sex, no sleep, no beer, no cigarettes.

He might as well work.

Joe tapped another search word into his computer, compiling his sources and statistics on the uninsured and underinsured of Chicago.

It's not about statistics, Nell objected in his memory. *My patients aren't numbers. They're people.*

Maybe people made an issue a story. Joe book-

marked a site on emergency-room costs at Chicago
Memorial. But numbers made it news.

And he was, or he had been, a decent newsman.

He stretched his neck. Cracked his knuckles. He'd
been at it for a couple of hours now. And Nell still
kept butting into his head. He still wanted her. She'd
imprinted herself on his body, impressed herself on
his brain.

That kiss… His blood surged heavily at the memory of her mouth, moving and hot on his, of her
breasts, full and soft, of her belly cradling his erection.

Okay, he was really uncomfortable now.

To distract himself, he typed "Burdett" into his
search engine. He wasn't really investigating her. He
was just curious. Anyway, he thought with a flash of
resentment, she sure as hell hadn't shown any scru-
ples about digging into his personal life.

A list of links appeared on his computer screen,
with the name highlighted and the context suggested.

He skimmed through the data. Most references
cited Sir Francis Burdett, an eighteenth-century member of Parliament. Joe scrolled down the list. He
didn't really associate Nell with British nobility. But
the family got around. There was a Burdett high
school in Kansas, a Burdett bed-and-breakfast in New
York, a Burdett cemetery in West Virginia.

None of it any use to him, unless Nell's ex was
buried there.

Joe added "Illinois" to his search criteria and
scanned the results: an architect who'd designed a
building on Wabash, a toastmaster, a teacher. A Burdett had graduated from Northwestern University
Medical School in 1994 and was currently on the staff

of Chicago Memorial. Joe's interest pricked. Nell's husband. Had to be.

He glanced farther down the list. There was a student essay written about the original Francis Burdett. A Web site for a Burdett's Bookstore in Elgin. A news story from a couple of years ago citing a settlement conference between an Eleanor Burdett and the Illinois state licensing board.

Whoa. Joe's pulse kicked. Rewind. Replay. What was that last one?

He clicked on the link.

And there it was, a headline from Chicago's other daily, the *Examiner's* rival paper: *State Ignores Guilty Nurses: Inadequate Controls for Medical Misconduct.*

Joe sucked in his breath and started reading.

The article was an account of the Illinois Department of Professional Regulation's lenient handling of nurses accused of negligence or incompetence. The state agency, in its attempts to keep pace with the nursing shortage and to provide troubled nurses with needed medical help, had a history of settling cases involving medication errors, petty theft, even abuse.

Joe's head pounded. His mouth was as dry as if he was coming off a three-day bender. The reporter had done her homework. She cited instances of nurses who defaulted on their school loans, nurses who stole drugs from patients to feed their own addictions, nurses who made fatal mistakes on the job.

Joe's mind, his heart, his stomach revolted. These stories had nothing to do with Nell. Not the Nell he knew.

But buried three subheadings down, in a paragraph taking the DPR to task for failing to report nurses suspected of committing felonies to the state's attorney's office, was the case of Eleanor Burdett.

Hell.

My husband's name was Burdett, Nell had confided to his mother.

Eleanor Burdett, the article stated, resigned from Chicago Memorial Hospital amid accusations of diverting prescription drugs.

Could it possibly…?

Could she possibly…?

Joe set his jaw and reread the paragraph. Phrases leapt out at him. *Superficial investigation. Token punishment.* Burdett's case had been plea-bargained, her disciplinary file purged of incriminating details, and Burdett herself placed on a three-year probation and allowed to return to work.

Our volunteer physicians are dedicated to our patients' care, Nell had said their first evening together.

Is that the company line? Joe had teased.

It's the truth.

Maybe. Or maybe all you doctors stick together.

Joe's gut churned. How had everybody missed this? How had he missed this?

He checked the dateline. The story was two years old. Okay, two years ago, he was talking to hostile locals in the Hindu Kush mountains, his brother Mike was fresh out of academy, the features editor at the *Examiner* was working for some paper in Wisconsin, and Nell…

More memories sliced through him. Everything she'd said, everything he'd believed her to be, was suddenly called into question.

What did you do before? he'd asked her that night at Flynn's.

I was a trauma nurse.

Where?

Her hands tightened around her beer mug. Does it matter?

I don't know. Why did you leave? It can't have been the money.

The shaking in his stomach stopped, replaced by a cold, sick certainty. Two years ago, Nell Dolan had been working at Chicago Memorial Hospital, where her husband was on staff.

The Eleanor Burdett in the article was her. Had to be her.

She'd left in disgrace and buried herself at a hole-in-the-wall clinic on the North Side because no reputable hospital would have her.

Her wide, clear eyes met his in appeal.

Can't you accept that some people are motivated by a simple desire to help?

Nope.

He'd been right about her all along. The thought should have made him happy. Nobody fooled Joe Reilly. Big, bad cynical reporter believes the worst and is proven right again.

Only he didn't want to be right.

Joe read the paragraph again. Eleanor Burdett had resigned from her hospital job after she was accused of diverting drugs.

For her own use? Or to sell?

Joe scowled. Nell sure as hell didn't act like a user. At least, he hadn't observed the signs, chronic lateness or difficulty concentrating, mood swings or deteriorating hygiene. She seemed genuinely responsible for her patients and competent at her job.

But he knew better than anyone that a junkie could

continue to function on a professional level even after his personal life had gone to hell.

Of course, it was possible that in the past two years Nell had turned her life around. Wasn't that what he was supposed to believe? *That a Power greater than ourselves could restore us to sanity?*

So maybe she wasn't an addict. Maybe she was only a phony.

And maybe she was a felon.

Drugs were missing from the clinic pharmacy. His brother Mike claimed the number of prescription drugs on the street had spiked, and at least one fraudulent prescription had turned up with Nell's name on it.

Mike's teasing voice came back to him. *Maybe you'll write the big story—Nurse Dolan Does Drug Diversion on the North Side.*

Joe stared at the damning words on the screen, his eyes burning. How did he explain to his brother that his big story had already appeared in a rival paper two years ago? Nell Dolan's personal failure and professional misconduct were old news.

But Joe still had a responsibility to share the story with the police. Didn't he? He still had to face Nell herself.

His stomach balled.

Sleep on that.

Nell glanced out at the rain streaking the clinic's front windows. She had enough to do this morning without worrying about Joe Reilly.

The waiting room steamed with wet shoes and drying umbrellas, stunk with sweat and misery, Betadine and pine cleaner. The doormat was saturated, the linoleum was slippery, the board by the nurses' station was already full, and Melody King was late.

Joe was not her problem.

He didn't want to be her problem.

He'd told her flat-out he didn't want her help.

And that, Nell admitted ruefully as she grabbed another chart, *was* her problem. She didn't see Joe as a patient, exactly; she just couldn't see herself as anything but a nurse. She didn't know how to have a relationship where she wasn't the one helping, giving, supporting. It was what she was good at. What she understood.

By rejecting her help, Joe was rejecting her. What else did she have to offer him?

Besides sex.

She had a sudden memory of Joe's hot, hooded eyes and lean, hard body and flushed. She was not having sex with a man who put restrictions up front on their relationship. That didn't mean she didn't think about it.

The waiting room was starting to resemble O'Hare airport, with patients jostling in line or circling like planes stacked up ready to land. Babies cried. Children ran between the chairs. Where the hell was Melody?

"I've got to see a doctor now," a man with a grizzled ponytail and hands the size of suitcases was insisting to Lucy Morales at the front desk.

Dark-haired Lucy was unimpressed. "We have to see our regularly scheduled appointments, Mr. Jones. But we will fit you in if you sit down."

"I can't sit down," Nell heard him complaining as she headed down the hall. "Damn it, my back hurts."

Nell ducked into the examining room, where an

elderly woman blushed and whispered all the classic symptoms of urinary tract infection. Nell patted her shoulder and explained the need for a urine sample.

"Just to be sure," she said with a smile. "And then we can get you some antibiotics for the infection and some Pyridium to make you feel better."

She left the woman clutching a specimen cup and went to the board to check her next appointment. Stanley Vacek. Nell frowned. Did the elderly Czech need his blood pressure medication adjusted again? Or was he simply lonely?

Somebody had tracked water in the work lane. Nell stooped to wipe it up. The last thing the clinic needed was for a patient to slip and break a hip.

Straightening, she saw Melody at her desk. Her hair hung in damp strands around her face. Beneath her pale blue lids, her eyes were red and puffy.

Nell frowned in concern. "Are you all right?"

Melody sniffled. "I have a little cold. And Rose—" Rose was her three-year-old "—didn't want to put on her shoes, and it's raining, and the bus was late…"

Nell nodded sympathetically, half listening to the familiar complaints, restraining herself from pointing out that illness, children and the vagaries of public transportation hadn't stopped most of their patients from showing up promptly at eight o'clock.

The rain did make everything worse, she thought, making an extra effort to be understanding because she didn't feel particularly understanding. She was tired, too. A combination of sit-up-in-the-dark fears and twist-in-the-sheets frustration had kept her up most of the night.

But Melody, poor Melody, looked awful. Despite

the humid, overheated air, she was shivering. Her eyes were glassy and her nose was running. She looked like someone in the grip of a very bad cold.

Or drug withdrawal.

The thought hit Nell like a slap. Sudden. Hard. Unavoidable. She sucked in her breath.

She didn't want to suspect Melody. She didn't want to suspect anybody. And of all the clinic's staff, the office manager had the least reason to go into the pharmacy and the best possible motivation for staying away.

"The problem with the Velcro shoes is Rose can take them off herself," Melody said, ignoring the large man jockeying for her attention on the other side of the counter. Mr. Back Pain, Nell remembered. Obviously, Lucy hadn't convinced him to wait. "She's so smart. So I told her…"

No, Nell couldn't bear to think of Rose's mommy doing or dealing drugs. It was just her own ghosts that made her see specters everywhere.

But the doubt, once raised, haunted her.

Melody's desk was right across from the pharmacy. She did have access to the clinic's patient list and to the locked drawer that held all the practitioners' prescription pads. She must have seen Nell's signature hundreds of times.

"You got to help me," the man interrupted, leaning over the counter. "I understand if the doctors are too busy to see me. All I need is a prescription refill."

Melody's blue eyelids fluttered. "Did you sign in, Mr., uh…?"

"Jones. Roy Jones." His thick finger stabbed the clipboard on the counter. "Right there."

"And do you have an appointment, Mr. Jones?"

His face darkened. "I told you. I don't need an appointment. But you've got to give me something for this pain."

His insistence made the hair stand up on the nape of Nell's neck.

More ghosts, she told herself firmly. She had no reason—yet—to suspect his demand. And rain and pain could make anybody cranky.

But instead of letting Melody handle it, she found herself moving forward. "Who's your doctor, Mr. Jones?"

He swung his grizzled head toward her like a bull scenting the matador. Nell resisted the urge to step back.

"I seen Dr. Graham before."

That at least sounded right. Orthopedist Chuck Graham volunteered at the clinic one Wednesday a month, fall and winter, when his altruism didn't interfere with his golf game.

Nell pasted on a smile. "I'm sorry, Dr. Graham isn't in today. But we should have your medical file. If you'd like to take a seat in the waiting room—"

"I've had a seat." His voice was loud enough to attract attention. Several patients looked over, and one moved away. "I can't sit no more. My back is killing me."

"All right," Nell said brightly. "One of the nurses will find your chart, and we'll try to get you into a room as soon as possible."

Before he scared away every soul in the waiting room.

Lucy Morales caught Nell's eye and mouthed a message.

Nell's heart sank.

"Would you excuse me a minute?" She left Jones looming over the desk, and went to speak to the other nurse.

"What is it?"

"No chart," Lucy said. "He's not a patient here."

Oh, God, she was tired. She so didn't want to have to deal with this. "Could he have seen Graham at his practice in Winnetka?"

They both looked back at Roy Jones, the stubby ponytail, the steel-toed boots, the sweat-stained shirt.

"He doesn't look like he could afford the bus fare to Winnetka," Lucy said frankly. "Let alone the specialist's fees when he got there."

Nell sighed. "Let's call, just the same. Maybe he has workmen's comp or something…"

But she wasn't surprised when Dr. Graham's receptionist insisted her office had no record of Roy Jones.

"What am I supposed to tell him?" Melody asked, her thin face worried.

Nell squeezed her shoulder in reassurance. "It's okay. I'll talk to him."

Because maybe she could help. Not only Melody, who was so clearly reluctant to go another round with the belligerent Jones. No, Nell was fool enough to hope she could help Jones himself.

Because he needed her help. Roy Jones exhibited the classic signs of a "doctor shopper," a drug seeker. And without her help, Roy Jones had no hope at all.

Taking a deep breath, Nell pushed open the door to the crowded waiting room. She was aware of other patients, swirls of movement, eddies of sound, the flow around the front entrance. But her attention fixed on Roy Jones, his sweaty face, his darting eyes, the clenching and unclenching of his big hands.

He was nervous.

The observation bolstered her. The clinic was her turf, her place, the place where she was in control, where she had the tools to be effective and the authority to do some good. She couldn't always control the course of a disease, couldn't always win the battle against pain and suffering. But here, at least, she knew where the battle lines were drawn. Here she was allowed to fight.

"Mr. Jones?" She smiled at him. "Would you come with me, please?"

His head thrust forward. "Why?"

"I'd like to do a physical examination. For your back problem."

"I don't need a physical examination." He added a filthy epithet. "Especially from some woman. All I need is my medication."

Something moved in the corner of Nell's vision, but she kept her gaze focused on Jones. Look away from the bull, and it trampled you.

"I don't know what to prescribe for you until you've been seen," she said evenly.

"*I* know. Dr. Graham always gives me Oxycontin. Or Percocet."

Schedule Two narcotics. Well, that took care of any last doubts she might have had about what Jones wanted.

"I'm not allowed to prescribe those drugs for you," Nell said. His eyes were wild. "But there are some nonnarcotic analgesics that might work for you." She took a step forward, willing him to let her reach him. To let her help him. "Why don't we go ahead with the examination to determine if there's a physical cause before we—''

''Examine this, bitch!'' Jones planted his big, meaty hand over her face and shoved.

Nell's head snapped back. Her arms flailed. She stumbled. And then her foot slid on a wet patch of linoleum and shot out from under her.

She went down like a stone. Hard, on her back. Her skull cracked against the floor with enough force to rattle her jaw and detonate stars.

Oh, God, that hurt.

''Nell!''

''Señorita?''

A babble of voices crashed over her, a tide of concern, a wave of activity. She struggled to surface, to force her heavy eyes to open, her weighted lips to move.

''Jones?'' she croaked.

''Ran out through the front door.'' This voice was male, grim and reassuringly familiar. ''Don't worry. I called the police.''

''No police,'' she tried to say. ''Not his fault. Mine.''

But she wasn't sure anyone could hear her. The ringing in her ears was very loud.

Someone was calling her name again, roughly, urgently. She was lying on the floor. She wanted to explain she would get up in a minute, in just a minute when she wasn't so tired.

A warm hand touched her face, cupped her jaw. She turned her cheek into the palm, instinctively seeking comfort.

''Don't move,'' the voice ordered. Joe's voice. The

cuff of his shirt brushed her nose. He smelled of mints and tobacco. "Can somebody get a damn doctor?"

Nell tried to remember who was on the schedule for today, but her mind refused to cooperate. Jim Fletcher? Susan Nguyen? No, Sue didn't come in until after lunch.

"You're supposed to ask me my name," she said, forcing the words from her thick tongue. "And the name of the president."

Joe swore. "I know your name. What I can't figure out is what the hell you thought you were doing taking on a junkie twice your size."

She smiled, keeping her eyes closed. It was kind of restful here on the floor. If only her head didn't hurt. "Trying to help," she explained.

"Yeah, that's a problem for you," Joe said dryly.

"Nell, my God, girl." That was Billie's voice, sharp with anxiety.

There was a rush behind her, a shift around her. The floor vibrated with running footsteps. Someone tugged on Nell's upper eyelid and shone a light in her eyes. She tried to pull back from the brightness and groaned as her head bumped the floor.

"Easy," Joe said, and was ignored.

Nell's friends, her co-workers, pressed around her. Don't leave me, Nell wanted to say.

But of course he would.

Chapter 9

"You don't have to stay." Nell sorted through the keys in her hand. "I'll be fine by myself."

"Not according to George Clooney." Joe took the keys and unlocked her door himself.

He didn't care what she said, she looked like hell. Her face was white as paper, and she had great big circles like ink smudges under her eyes.

She blinked at him. "Who?"

Maybe she was still disoriented from that crack on the head.

Joe held the door open. "George Clooney. Dr. Kildare. The guy in the lab coat who checked out your head and various other body parts."

Okay, so he was jealous. He was burning with jealousy, and that pissed him off and panicked him at the same time. But it was nothing, *nothing,* compared to the gut-clenching terror he'd felt when Nell's head hit the floor.

Her face cleared. "Jim Fletcher. He's one of our
volunteer pediatricians." She started to feel her way
down the hall, one hand on the wall for balance like
a drunk. "Dr. Jim thinks all of his patients need to
have their hands held. Which they do, since they're
mostly under ten years old. But I'm a big girl. I'm
used to taking care of myself."

"Yeah, I got that," Joe muttered, following her.

And that was another thing that pissed him off.
Didn't she have family she could call? Didn't she
have friends who could take a few hours away from
their own lives to make sure she was okay?

His own family made him crazy, but at least Joe
had never had to depend on, well, on somebody like
him to get him through the night.

Nell stopped and swayed in the middle of her living
room, lacing her fingers together like a child. "I'm
sorry you got stuck with me," she said in a small
voice. "Really, I'll be fine."

"Don't be stupid," Joe snapped.

No, that was wrong. He didn't have any experience
with nursing, but he was pretty sure he wasn't supposed to yell at a patient with a concussion. What
would his mother do?

"Do you want some soup?" he asked.

Nell studied him, her gaze soft and considering,
until he was the one who felt dizzy.

"You make soup?" she asked at last.

"Hell, no," he said, his horror only half-feigned.
"But I can heat it if it comes in a can."

Her smile bloomed, making his breath catch.

"I appreciate the offer. But—"

"Look, I owe you, okay?" he growled. "Let me
do this, and we can call it even."

PLAY
Lucky 7

and get **2 FREE BOOKS** and a **FREE GIFT**

Scratch off the gold area with a coin. Then check below to see the gifts you get!

NO COST! NO OBLIGATION TO BUY!
NO PURCHASE NECESSARY!

YES!

I have scratched off the gold area. Please send me the **2 FREE BOOKS AND GIFT** for which I qualify. I understand I am under no obligation to purchase any books as explained on the back of this card.

345 SDL DZ4Y

245 SDL DZ5F

FIRST NAME

LAST NAME

ADDRESS

APT #

CITY

STATE/PROV.

ZIP/POSTAL CODE

(S-IM-04/04)

| 7 | 7 | 7 | Worth **2 FREE BOOKS** plus a **FREE GIFT!** |

Worth **2 FREE BOOKS!**

Worth **1 FREE BOOK!**

Try Again!

The Silhouette Reader Service™ — Here's how it works:

Accepting your 2 free books and gift places you under no obligation to buy anything. You may keep the books and gift and return the shipping statement marked "cancel." If you do not cancel, about a month later we'll send you 6 additional books and bill you just $3.99 each in the U.S., or $4.74 each in Canada, plus 25¢ shipping & handling per book and applicable taxes if any.* That's the complete price and — compared to cover prices of $4.75 each in the U.S. and $5.75 each in Canada — it's quite a bargain! You may cancel at any time, but if you choose to continue, every month we'll send you 6 more books, which you may either purchase at the discount price or return to us and cancel your subscription.

*Terms and prices subject to change without notice. Sales tax applicable in N.Y. Canadian residents will be charged applicable provincial taxes and GST.

Her forehead creased. "Owe me for what?"

For believing you could be a phony. A felon. A thief.

Nope, he couldn't say that.

"For being a jackass the other night." He came closer, close enough to see the tiny lines at the corners of her eyes, to smell the clean, subtle scent of her, soap and skin. "Let me make it up to you."

She looked away, color moving into her face. "Really, I'm fine. All I need is a nap."

He wanted to lie down with her. He wanted to help her out of her clothes, her crumpled white lab coat and her soft green sweater, and stroke her and comfort her and…

Joe jerked his mind back from that little fantasy and tried to remember where naps fell on Dr. Kildare's list of warnings and instructions. Rest was good. Loss of consciousness was bad. Sleep was good. Abnormally deep sleep or difficulty waking was bad. Check the patient's responses every hour to ensure there was no bleeding or swelling in or around the brain.

"A nap's okay." And then some demon made him add, "You want me to tuck you in?"

She smiled again, but ruefully. "I want you to go home."

She didn't get it.

Hell, he didn't get it, either. But he couldn't leave her.

He was a seasoned foreign correspondent, for God's sake. He'd seen soldiers die in ambush and women blown to pieces while they waited for the bus. But it still tore him up inside that Nell had been assaulted in her own clinic for trying to save some low-life bastard from the consequences of his own bad choices.

"Not happening, babe," he said roughly. "Deal with it."

Nell raised her eyebrows. "Is that your best bed-side manner? 'Deal with it'?"

"You want to see my bedside manner, stick around. You want to take a nap, haul your cute little butt to bed now."

"I'm touched," Nell said.

He scowled at her.

"And grateful."

She stood on tiptoe to press warm lips to his jaw. He went dumb as a rock and hard as stone.

"There's beer and soda in the fridge," she said. "Make yourself at home."

He watched her retreat down the hall with the care-ful steps of a DUI walking the line beside the high-way and had to shove his hands in his pockets so he didn't grab her and haul her back into his arms.

He needed that beer.

He needed a meeting.

She needed him sober and here.

Taking a deep breath, Joe went to get a something to drink from her nearly empty refrigerator.

Popping the seal on a can of soda, he hobbled back to the living room. He hadn't seen much of Nell's apartment before. Just the hall, and then he'd been so hot to nail her against the wall he hadn't paid atten-tion to her taste in interior decoration.

Not that it looked like Nell did much decorating. Her furniture looked like his, the battered belongings of someone who didn't expect to be home very often. But scattered through the room were splotches of color, touches of comfort: a reading lamp by an over-stuffed chair, fat candles burned to various lengths, a soft red throw draped over a couch.

Books crammed low shelves under the windows, paperback romances and medical texts mostly. He bent to scan the titles. Passions. Dreams. Virgins. Daddies.

Joe grinned. Nurse Dolan had one hell of a fantasy life.

The shelf below wasn't nearly as much fun. Text-books, some with yellow "used" stickers still on the spines. A half-dozen guides and dictionaries to diagnoses, interventions and collaborative care. Four different drug handbooks, a stack of nursing journals, some psychology texts and self-help books about addiction.

He didn't want to see those.

He wasn't looking for them.

But there were a lot—weren't there?—compared to the other medical books. Only two on trauma care, for instance, and one on infectious diseases...

He pushed away from the book shelf so suddenly he staggered, sick at heart and in his gut. Furious with himself for looking. For caring. For suspecting her. Again.

He hadn't brought Nell home to poke through her possessions like some tabloid reporter sifting through celebrity garbage. He was here to take care of her, damn it.

There had to be something he could do to validate his presence in her home, in her life. Restless, he roamed back to the kitchen and got another soda from the fridge. Limping down the hall, he tapped softly on her door.

Nothing.

That was okay. She was probably asleep. He stood there, the cold glass sweating in his hand. Or she'd gotten up to use the bathroom. She could have passed out crossing the rug. Or fallen down on the cold tiles. Or…

Quietly, cursing himself for a fool, he opened the door.

She was asleep, neatly folded into herself under the covers. In the light that filtered around the edges of the shade, he could see her dark eyebrows and pale hair, the curve of her hip, the slope of her shoulder. One hand rested palm up on her pillow, fingers curled in like the petals of a flower. The other clutched her blanket to her chin.

Her mouth was open.

Such a minor thing, such a human thing, to make his heart pound and tenderness punch his chest.

Her face was soft and unprotected. Whatever Nell was hiding, whatever she was guarding, in sleep her face relaxed into innocence.

She snored faintly.

And he wanted, more fiercely than he'd wanted anything in his wandering life, to shuck his pants and his pretenses and crawl under that blanket with her. To kiss her soft, half-open mouth. To cup her face, smooth with sleep. To stroke and explore her warm, relaxed body, to feel those neat, nurse's hands touching him.

Yeah, he wanted that. Bad.

Grimly, he set the glass and the soda on her nightstand and went back to the living room to watch CNN.

* * *

Nell woke to the sound of male voices in the other room and the smell of something wonderful cooking in her apartment. Both were so unusual that she lay still for a long moment, convinced she was still dreaming.

Lovely, hot, delirious dreams of Joe.

Her room was dim. Her head hurt, and she had to use the bathroom. Not dreaming, then. Just delirious.

She eased to a sitting position and tested her feet on the floor. Steady enough.

Reaching for the lamp switch, she spotted a glass with an inch of water and an unopened can of soda waiting by her bed.

Her breath caught. *Joe.*

That was his voice she heard in her living room. She'd fallen—no, she'd been pushed and hit her head, and Joe had brought her home and watched over her as she slept.

The image stirred her. Disturbed her.

She shuffled into the bathroom. Well, anybody would be a little freaked to find the man she'd just made love to in her dreams watching TV in her living room. But Nell was even more unsettled by her own reaction.

She was glad he hadn't gone.

She liked her independence. Didn't she? She protected her privacy. She'd trained herself to rely only on herself. At least that way when she was disappointed she had only herself to blame. The last thing she needed was to start depending on a man who refused to accept her help in return.

So why were her eyes in the mirror so bright?

Nell bit her lip and leaned over the sink, peering

closer at her pupils. At least they were the right size. And there was no bruising or discoloration around her eyes or behind her ears to suggest a dangerous subdural hematoma.

She twisted her neck and explored the back of her skull cautiously with her fingers. Ouch. Okay, she had a nice-sized goose egg there. But she didn't appear to be bleeding. Really, she was doing just fine. There was no reason—no medical reason at all—for Joe to stay.

Depressed, she pulled on her robe and went to tell him so.

Mike Reilly was in her living room, wearing his uniform and watching ESPN on her TV.

Nell stopped dead in the doorway, one hand clutching the neckline of her robe.

Mike looked up and raised a long-necked bottle of beer in salute. "Hi, Nell. How's the head?"

Throbbing.

Confused. Was he here as Joe's brother? Or as the beat cop investigating…What was he investigating?

Nell tugged on the belt of her robe. "It's— I'm fine, thanks."

"You don't look fine." Joe appeared in the arch that separated the living room from the kitchen. His sharp blue eyes narrowed in concern. "Are you dizzy? Nauseous?"

Nell curled her bare toes into the carpet, uncomfortably aware that both men were assessing her, her pale face, her wrecked hair, her ratty green robe…

She attempted a smile, praying it didn't look as stiff as it felt. "No, I'm hungry, actually."

"Good." Joe crossed the room and cupped her upper arms. She managed not to jump in surprise. He tugged her closer, so that her breasts leaned into his chest, and brushed a kiss to her forehead. Her heart melted. Just for a second, woozy and weak with pain and longing, she let her eyes drift closed.

Joe's mouth moved against her hairline. "Mike brought dinner."

Nell opened her eyes to find Joe's brother watching them with undisguised interest from the couch.

She felt her space invaded, her privacy intruded on, and cleared her throat. "I wondered what you were doing here."

"Ma made you some *pasta e fagioli*." Mike's smile didn't quite reach his eyes. "And I figured as long as I was here, I could take your statement."

"Later," Joe said.

"No, it's all right." Nell pulled herself from his arms, trying not to miss his warmth, trying to draw her scattered thoughts together. Trying not to resent the way her home had been taken over while she slept. "What statement?"

"We're still looking for the guy who attacked you," Mike said. "Joe gave us a description, but it would help us if we had a statement from you."

Nell moistened her dry lips. "Nobody attacked me. I fell."

"That son of a bitch knocked you down," Joe said.

"He pushed me out of the way," Nell corrected. "And I slipped. I should have been more careful. I could see he was upset."

"Why the hell are you defending him?"

"Did he have any reason to believe he would be successful in obtaining drugs from your clinic?" Mike asked.

It was a cop's question.

But he'd brought her *soup,* Nell thought rather desperately.

She blinked. "Excuse me?"

"Did you know him?" Mike clarified.

When had Joe's brother taken out his notebook?

"No, I—"

"She just got up," Joe interrupted. "She hit her head. She's confused. Can't we do this later?"

"You're the one who wanted to go after this guy," Mike said.

"I am not confused," Nell said. But she was starting to get ticked off. "No, I'd never seen this patient before. That's why I asked Melody to contact Dr. Graham's office and get a history. And I'm happy to give you a description to circulate to other doctors and hospitals in the area. Mr. Jones obviously needs help. But—"

"Told you so," Joe said to his brother.

"But—" Nell raised her voice "—I won't press charges against him if you do find him."

The Reilly brothers, the reporter and the cop, leveled near identical scowls in her direction. Nell would have found it funny if her head hadn't hurt so much.

She could accept the duality of their roles as long as they respected hers. She wasn't just a victim. She was a nurse. And she took the responsibilities of her job every bit as seriously as Mike took his. More.

"Why not?" demanded Joe. "He pushed you down."

"Because he felt threatened," Nell insisted.

"That's bull," Joe said. "He's the one who threatened you. Mike should bust his ass."

Nell crossed her arms over the front of her shabby green robe. Her head pounded and her ears were ringing, but she was not going down. "And if I set the police on every patient who pushed me or threatened me, how long do you think I'd keep the respect of this community? I need my patients' trust. And I'm not losing it because one guy got aggressive in the waiting room."

Mike scratched his head with his pen. "You do know this guy is a con, right? A druggie. A doctor shopper."

"No, I don't know that," Nell said. "It's certainly one explanation for his behavior. Or he could have developed a drug tolerance and truly been in need of a new prescription to help him manage his pain. Without examining him, it's impossible for me to say. Or you, either."

"Are you telling me you would have prescribed drugs for this guy?"

"Back off, Mike," Joe said quietly. "I told you she didn't. She has the bump on her head to prove it."

She should let it go, Nell thought desperately. She was already a suspect for the pharmacy thefts and prescription-drug fraud. Her reputation, her license, maybe even her freedom were on the line.

Joe was willing to defend her. Mike might be willing to believe her.

If she had any sense of self-preservation at all, she would let it go.

Her head pounded.

Damn it, Dolan, don't you ever give up?

I want to… It's not an option.

"Yes, I would have written a prescription for some appropriate medication," Nell said carefully. "If a physical examination established that the patient needed them.''

Joe looked at her thoughtfully.

Mike snorted. ''Of course he needed them. He's an addict.''

Nell sighed. ''Not necessarily. Pain and the fear of pain can cause a pseudoaddiction—behavior that mimics an actual physical or psychological dependence on drugs because the patient is desperate to avoid or alleviate real suffering.''

''You sure know an awful lot about addicts,'' Mike said.

The line she was walking between her professional obligations and her personal life blurred. Nell looked from Mike to Joe, unsure of her footing, afraid she was about to take a fall.

Or a leap of faith.

She tightened her hands on the belt of her robe to hide their trembling. ''I should,'' she said. ''I was married to one.''

Chapter 10

Joe had protected sources before. But never from his own brother.

"You certainly got rid of him in a hurry," Nell remarked, sitting sideways at the kitchen table. She crossed her legs, and her robe slipped open at the knee.

Hello. Joe hadn't seen her legs before. She always wore slacks. Against the dark green terry cloth, her skin looked pale and soft. Her knees were round. Bare.

He slopped soup onto the table and swore.

Nell sat up in concern. "Did you burn yourself?"

She was too quick to take care of everybody else. It was time somebody took care of her.

"No. Sit. I've got it."

God help them both.

He ladled beans and noodles into two bowls, trying not to stare at her smooth, bare knees.

Knees. He shook his head. Man, that was pathetic.

"Mmm." Nell inhaled steam, closing her eyes briefly in appreciation. "This smells wonderful. Your mother shouldn't have gone to all this trouble."

Joe sat opposite her, careful to angle his legs so they weren't touching hers. "Are you kidding? She wanted to bring it herself, but I talked her out of it. I figured you weren't ready yet for Ma in full Irish-mother mode."

Nell arched her brows. "But you thought I was ready for your brother in full Irish-cop mode?"

Regret sliced through him.

"No, I pretty much wasn't thinking at all on that one," he admitted. "I wanted the guy who hurt you caught."

Nell smiled and ate her soup. With her mouth full, she couldn't talk. Joe wondered if that was deliberate.

He waited until her bowl was nearly empty before he said, "Tell me about your ex-husband."

Nell swallowed. "I already gave a statement to your brother."

Score one for the nurse. Obviously, Nell wasn't handicapped by a little thing like a concussion.

"I heard your statement," Joe said. "I also heard what you left out."

"And like a good reporter, you decided now was a good time to get the whole story?"

But this wasn't about the story for Joe anymore. This was personal.

He held her gaze deliberately. "I figured this was a good time to share some of those details of our personal lives that you're so hot about."

The echoes of their last argument trembled between them.

Two people can't form a relationship without sharing some details of their personal lives.

How much sharing are you willing to do, Mrs. Burdett?

Nell's gaze dropped to her bowl. She didn't answer.

"Did you know your ex was using when you married him?" Joe persisted.

"Is this one of those 'when did you stop beating your wife' questions?"

He didn't laugh.

Nell sighed. "All right, no. I realize you think I have some save-the-world complex, but I didn't choose to get involved with a man who had a drug problem."

Joe winced. Well, he'd asked. "So, you didn't marry him to save him?"

She scraped her spoon against the bottom of her bowl. "I married Richard because he was brilliant and charming and he said he needed me."

Her eyes were distant. Joe wanted her here. With him.

"I missed that," Nell said softly. "Being needed. When I was growing up, my mother worked two dead-end jobs to support us, but she always made a big deal about how she needed me to keep things together at home."

Joe thought of Nell, awkward and willing, cutting carrots in the kitchen with his mother, and thought he understood. "What did she think of your husband?"

"She died before I could introduce them." Nell pushed her bowl away. "Richard was...there, you know? I guess I went from cooking and cleaning and doing her laundry to cooking and cleaning and doing his.''

Joe felt a flare of resentment toward her ex-husband, who had taken advantage of her grief and loneliness to move in on her.

''And what did Richard do while you were putting him through school and keeping house?''

Nell looked surprised. ''He was a resident,'' she said, as if that explained everything. And maybe, to her, it did. ''He was under enormous pressure. Practically living at the hospital. That's when he started using amphetamines to make it through his work rotations. Only then he couldn't sleep, and he'd have to take something else to come down. I tried to talk to him about it, but he said he was managing. He said he just needed a little help to make it through the last year.''

Her voice was strained. Joe wondered if all this revelation was too much for her, coming after her attack and on top of her near concussion. Not to mention his invasion of her home and his brother's badgering.

But he needed to know, if he was going to defend her. He wanted to know.

He reached across the table and took her hand. ''So, what happened?''

''I hoped when Richard received a permanent appointment in anesthesiology that things would get better. Maybe for a while they did. But then a friend of mine, an OR nurse, warned me he was using IV fentamyl. And he was wasting too much.''

Joe frowned. ''You mean wasted.''

''No. Morphine is dispensed in ten cc ampoules. If a patient's dosage is less than that, you push the required amount into his IV line and then push—waste—the rest into the garbage before you toss the syringe. You're supposed to have a witness,'' Nell explained. ''You call out, 'wasting,' and then you do it. Only Richard was calling and then pocketing the half-full syringe.''

''Clever,'' Joe said.

''Common,'' Nell corrected.

She would know.

''What did you do?''

''I told him to get help,'' Nell said, using small words and short sentences, as if that would somehow help her get through this. ''I threatened to report him. He promised to stop.''

And of course Nell had believed him. Nell believed in everybody. Which either made her the biggest sap in the world or the angel her patients called her.

''But he didn't,'' Joe said.

''I thought he did. We worked in the same hospital. We had friends... My spies, he called them. I thought it would help.'' Her throat moved as she swallowed. Her fingers tightened on his. ''And then one day the hospital chief of staff called me into his office when I came off shift and demanded to know why I was writing prescriptions to supply my husband's drug habit.''

''That's bull,'' Joe growled.

Nell smiled wryly. ''Well, yes. But I understood how he could reach that conclusion. Apparently Richard was using my prescription pad and forging my signature.''

Mike's voice echoed in Joe's head like mortar fire.

The nurse? We got called to her clinic because she was writing bad prescriptions... She's saying some-

*body either photocopied an old prescription or stole
her prescription pad and forged her signature.*

That happens, doesn't it?

Happens all the time.

"Did you tell this guy—the chief of staff—did you
tell him what you suspected?"

"Oh, yes." Her hand was cold in his. "But he said
that if he believed me he had no choice but to fire
Richard. If, on the other hand, I was willing to take
responsibility for diverting drugs from the hospital
pharmacy, he would see to it that Richard kept his
job and received treatment for his drug problem."

She pulled back her hand and folded her napkin
precisely into quarters. "It seemed the best solution
at the time."

Joe kept his voice level with an effort. "The best
solution for Richard. What about you?"

"Oh." Nell sat back, blinking, as if he'd introduced some radical new variable into her neat for-
mula. "Well, DPR—the Illinois Department of Professional Regulation—only requires hospitals to
notify them if a nurse is fired. Not if she resigns."

Cold settled in Joe's stomach.

She wouldn't, he thought. Nobody could be that
conscientious. That self-sacrificing. That stupid.

Nobody except maybe the Angel of Ark Street.

"You resigned," he said flatly.

Nell gave a small nod. "I didn't want to continue
to work in the same hospital anymore anyway. But
one of Richard's colleagues filed a complaint with the
Nursing Board."

"For God's sake, *why?*"

Nell lined up her spoon precisely with the edge of
the table. "I'm not sure."

But Joe could guess. After Nell's ex was forced into treatment by the hospital's chief of staff, he must have been anxious to pin his misconduct on somebody. And who better than his eager-to-take-responsibility ex-wife?

Selfish, slimy, son of a bitch.

"So they held a private settlement conference and put you on probation," Joe concluded grimly.

Nell's clear blue eyes widened. "How did you know?"

Her question caught him like a camera flash. And the picture he got of himself wasn't pretty.

Hell. Joe got up to carry their bowls to the sink. What should he tell her?

Honesty is the best policy, Mary Reilly used to tell her sons.

The truth will set you free. That was in the Bible.

But Joe the journalist didn't believe in truth anymore. Not when the facts in this case could send Nell to jail. Not when confessing what he'd done could wreck his chances of taking her to bed. He never should have opened his mouth to his brother. He wasn't going to compound his error by blabbing to Nell now.

Anyway, it wasn't fair to her—was it?—to make her worry about what he knew or what he'd found out. Especially since he didn't intend to do anything with the information.

Except tell his brother to bury it.

Joe rinsed the bowls under the tap. "It's obvious the hospital would want to hush things up." Smooth, Reilly. Very smooth. "And it figures the nursing board would have to impose some sanctions. I hope the son of a bitch was grateful."

"Richard? Not particularly."

Joe turned, his hands wet. "Tell me he at least came to your hearing," he begged.

"He was eager to put the past behind him," Nell said straight-faced. "His wife—did I mention he married the colleague who filed the complaint against me?—felt it would hurt his recovery to be under that much stress."

Anger sharpened his voice. "What about your stress?"

A week ago maybe he wouldn't have noticed the way her chin wobbled before she got it back under control. Maybe he wouldn't have seen the old hurt that darkened her eyes.

He noticed now, and it made him want somebody dead.

"I don't think Richard's wife was nearly as concerned about my stress levels," Nell said lightly.

"Somebody should have been."

"The chief of staff spoke up for me," Nell offered.

"He damn well should have, seeing as he got you to take the fall for his guy in the first place. Honey, you were screwed."

She opened her mouth to protest. Thought better of it and shrugged. "Possibly."

"Are you going to contact him now?"

She looked genuinely surprised. "Why?"

"To set the record straight."

"I suppose... No. What good would it do?"

"It would keep you from losing your license. It could keep you from going to jail."

She crossed her arms defensively. He watched the movement push her breasts together and thought, She isn't wearing a bra.

"I'm not going to jail," she said. "The only place I'm going now is to bed."

Oh, yeah. Bed was a great idea. They could solve all of their problems in bed.

Wrong.

Joe shoved his hands into his pockets. He was angry with Nell's user-abuser ex-husband, the jealous bitch who had reported her and the slick chief of staff who had sacrificed her to hospital expediency.

Mad at Nell for letting them get away with it.

And furious with himself. Because before tonight, he'd been just as willing as everybody else to use her.

He glared at her, sitting bare kneed and braless across the kitchen table.

The sooner he had her tucked into bed— alone— the better for both of them.

"Go to bed," he said. "I'll take the couch."

"Why?"

His heart beat faster. Did she mean…? Did she want…?

"I'm perfectly all right by myself," she continued.

Okay, she didn't want him. But she needed him, damn it.

"Yeah, you said. But your doctor said someone had to stay with you for at least twenty-four hours." Someone responsible, Fletcher had said, but sometimes you had to work with what you had. "And since you have the self-preservation instincts of a squirrel in the middle of the road, I think I'll stick around."

Joe's profile was sharp in the light from the door. His shoulders were big in shadow. He bent over the foot of Nell's bed, clumsily folding an ice-filled bag-

gie in a towel, caring and sweet and so grimly earnest
it made Nell want to cry.

She'd bared her soul to this man tonight, and he
wanted to put her to bed with an ice pack.

The dumbass.

"Okay, this should stay now." He approached the
head of the bed, the bundled package in his hand.
"Where do you, uh…"

She took it from him. He was trying so hard. "I'll
put it on when I lie down. Thank you."

"No problem." He stood a moment, shoulders
hunched. She held her breath in anticipation.

And then he leaned forward and quickly, gently,
kissed her cheek. "Good night."

She sat stunned, her heart wide open and her hands
clutching the covers. There was no time to absorb
him, to savor the rasp of his jaw or the brush of his
lips, to breathe in the blended scents of warm male
and hot soup.

He straightened. "You want anything else?"

Nell looked him right in the eye. "Yes. And I'm
not getting it."

He recoiled.

Too blunt, she thought, stricken. Too needy. Maybe
he would chalk it up to her head injury.

"Is something wrong?" he asked warily.

Her head throbbed. Her heart pounded.

She should tell him no.

She should let it go.

She should…

"You compared me to a squirrel," Nell said.

His eyes narrowed. "What are you talking about?"

"Not in a furry, appealing, come-find-the-nuts-in-
my-pocket way, either," Nell said, winding up.

''More in a get-out-of-the-road-before-you-get-hit-by-a-truck way. I'm not stupid.''

''I never said—''

''And I'm not weak.''

''No, you—''

''And I'm not an angel.''

''Nell…'' His voice shook with laughter and something else she was too upset to identify.

''I just told you all my darkest, dirtiest secrets, and you're still treating me like some poor baby you have to pat on the head and put to bed.''

He thrust his hands into his pockets. ''How am I supposed to treat you? You have a concussion. You need rest.''

Her throat ached. Her eyes burned. ''That's not all I need.''

Joe swore and sat on the side of her bed. The mattress dipped under his weight, tilting her toward him.

Pressure built, in her head and in her chest. She sniffed to keep it inside. ''I'm not crying.''

''Of course not.'' He put his arm around her, easing her forward until her head dropped on his hard shoulder.

''I never cry,'' she insisted, her voice muffled. Richard had hated to see her cry. And her mother had made her feel guilty.

Joe kissed the top of her head. ''You've had a rough day.''

''No, I…''

She didn't have rough days. She was the one who soothed and smoothed the way for everyone else.

''Go ahead. Let it out,'' Joe said. ''You're entitled.''

No one in her life had ever said those words to her.

Be a big girl, Eleanor.
Don't be selfish.
Don't make a fuss.
We're counting on you.

Her tears leaked into his shirt. Her nose was running. Her chest ached. Crying on him had to be the least seductive thing she could do. The thought depressed her even more. And yet she couldn't seem to stop.

Joe rubbed her back and murmured soft, senseless words into her hair as she choked and sobbed. Her fear and fatigue, her pain and failure came out in gasps and tears.

"I'm sorry," she mumbled.

"Shh. It's all right."

But it wasn't.

"I'm not usually such a nuisance."

"You mean, you suck at letting other people take care of you."

"I—"

"That's okay." He tucked her head more firmly under his chin. "I suck at taking care of people, so we both have something to get used to."

Her mind struggled with that. *Something to get used to.* Did he mean, tonight? Or was he actually implying he might stick around? But she didn't want to think about that now. Didn't want to contemplate the morning, when he'd be gone.

The average human body temperature was between ninety-seven and ninety-nine degrees. Joe felt warmer than that. Basking in his heat, Nell felt the tension seep from her neck, and then her shoulders. His damp shirt was rough under her cheek. His heart thudded under her ear. Gradually, she relaxed into him, into the strength of his arms and the support of his chest. They sat for long moments measured in breaths.

Nell sighed. "Actually, I think you're pretty good at taking care of—" she almost said "me" "—people."

His laughter stirred her hair. "Shows how little you know."

He stroked a strand from her forehead, carefully avoiding the bump on the back of her head. Her heart swelled.

"You think you could get some sleep now?" he asked.

"Could you—" She stopped.

He pulled back just enough to look at her. "What?"

Nell kept her chin lowered. She didn't want to face the reflection she might see in his eyes: her swollen eyes and blotchy face, her scarred heart and tarnished integrity, her failed marriage and shaky prospects.

She drew a breath, both for courage and because Joe seemed to be using up all the oxygen in the room.

She looked up. "Would you sleep with me?"

Chapter 11

Joe couldn't think.

All the blood that was supposed to supply his brain with oxygen surged straight to his groin, leaving him light-headed and hard as stone.

"You, uh, want to…"

Nell's color deepened in the yellow light from the hall. "You said you were going to sleep on the couch. I just thought… There's plenty of room in here. I thought you'd be more comfortable."

His mind was still playing catch-up.

Comfortable, next to?

Comfortable, on top of?

Comfortable buried as deep inside her as he could get, with her legs around his waist?

He tried to work moisture into his suddenly dry mouth. There was nothing he wanted more than to exploit this odd and intimate situation and take advantage of Nell's temporary weakness. And nothing he was more determined *not* to do.

"What about you?" he asked carefully. "What would make you comfortable?"

Her gaze slid from his. Her fingers plucked the satin binding at the edge of the blanket. "I'd like you to stay. I guess the incident this afternoon rattled me more than I thought."

"You took quite a hit," he said, trying not to picture her naked. "That doctor guy said you might not be thinking too straight for a while."

Which probably explained her willingness to sleep with him.

"I'm fine. It's just…I didn't have control of the situation, and I was…" Her voice trailed off.

Scared, Joe realized. Indomitable Nurse Dolan was hurt and scared.

He tightened his arm around her. "That makes two of us, then, babe, because when I saw you go down, I was terrified."

She looked at him and smiled, and that tentative curve of her lips loosed something warm in his chest that made him feel bigger. Made him feel better. Made him feel maybe he didn't suck at this comfort stuff after all.

He stood and unfastened his belt. "Left or right?"

She dragged her gaze from the zipper of his jeans. "Excuse me?"

Oh, man. "The bed. Which side do you take, left or right?"

"Oh." She shook her head at her own mistake and then winced. "Um…Right, I guess."

He looked over at her, at her round breasts and long thighs making bumps and valleys under the covers.

"You guess?" he repeated.

"I don't do this often enough to have a side," she confessed. "Mostly I sleep in the middle."

That would work. That would definitely work. If she got pressed for room in the night, maybe she'd climb on top of him.

Comfort, he reminded himself. Don't be a pig.

He sat on the edge of the mattress to untie his shoes.

Nell snuggled under the blanket, making the landscape dip and change. "Would you mind getting my pills from the bathroom?"

He paused in the act of jerking off one shoe, choking down his automatic protest. "What pills?"

"My head hurts."

"That's what the ice pack is for, sweet cakes. You shouldn't take—"

"—anything stronger than acetaminophen with a head injury," Nell finished for him, smiling. "I know. I've got a bottle in the medicine cabinet. Could you get me two, please?"

He exhaled in relief. "No problem."

And it wasn't really.

He fetched her pills—resisting his professional urge to inventory the contents of her medicine cabinet—and a glass of water and stood over her while she drank.

"All set?" he asked, taking her empty glass.

She nodded. "I really do appreciate this," she said in a small voice.

"It's nothing," he told her, because it was. She deserved better than this. She deserved better than him.

He unbuttoned his collar and cuffs and lay down

beside her, trying not to notice how his weight made her roll toward him. Under the blanket, things shifted in a very interesting way. Her round knees pressed his thigh through the covers.

Joe stared at the ceiling. Comfort, he told himself. Control.

Nell stirred. The sheets rustled. Joe held his breath as her hand with its short, neat, nurse's nails settled in the center of his chest. Very tentatively, her cheek came to rest against his shoulder. He swallowed, hard. He could smell her hair, the warm herbal notes of her shampoo and the sharper scent of whatever antiseptic they'd used on her scalp.

She sighed and slept.

After a long while, he did, too.

Nell woke up happy, which was different enough to alert her that something had happened even before she felt the throb in her head and felt Joe, warm and heavy beside her on the bed.

He was holding her hand.

She opened her eyes. He really was. Her right hand rested on his chest, and, sometime during the night, he had enclosed it in both of his, lacing his fingers with hers, holding her hand to his heart.

Tenderness surged inside her. She raised herself on her other elbow, studying him in the gray light that poked around the edges of the shade.

His face was hard and dark in sleep, his jaw stubbled, his mouth compressed. He looked like a man who lived with pain. Or secrets. Even his body was contained, controlled, his arms folded, his legs straight along the mattress.

He must be cold, after sleeping on top of the covers

all night. Poor guy. At least his skin felt warm enough. Nell slid her hand from his to pull up the blanket at the foot of the bed and noticed something else. Underneath the rough denim of his jeans, he was very aroused.

She blinked. Well. Wow. That was nice. Of course, morning arousal was common among men. She couldn't take it personally.

But she looked again anyway. Very nice.

Excitement uncurled in the pit of her stomach. Her pulse picked up speed. Not that she would do anything about it. Not that he would want her to. She glanced again at the fabric straining over his hips. Would he?

He'd been so careful with her last night. So kind.

She swallowed. Leaning more weight on her elbow, she let herself sink into him, greedy for the comfort of his physical presence, real and solid in her bed. She lowered her face until it almost touched his, until she felt his breath skate across her lips.

She would never have the nerve to do this if he was awake. But he wasn't. There was no one to see, no one to object, if she stole this moment for herself. If she stole one kiss. If this one time, after twenty-two months of nunlike existence, she was a little bit selfish. A little bit bad. Gently, testingly, she fit her mouth to his.

Warm. His lips were warm and firm, smooth and a little dry. She kissed him again, exploring, experimenting, letting her tongue dab delicately at the corner of his mouth, rubbing her lips over his, losing herself in his male textures, his male tastes. He tasted like sleep and sex and her toothpaste. He tasted delicious.

His mouth opened wider, and his arm came around to hold her. He angled his head, and the kiss changed, became hotter, wetter, deeper, wilder, a thing of tongues and teeth. He was awake, an active participant. She was no longer in control of their kiss.

Nell raised her head.

Joe was watching her, his blue eyes brilliant beneath hooded lids, his hard face flushed, his lips slick from her kisses. His breathing rasped. Her heart pounded.

She nearly strangled on embarrassment. After you'd practically inhaled a man in his sleep, what did you say?

She cleared her throat. "Good morning."

He smiled slowly. "Yeah, it is."

Heat clutched her. "I thought you were asleep," she mumbled.

"Was that it?" His eyes gleamed. "I wondered."

"Well." She struggled to regroup. Her body was heavy with languor, hollow with desire. "I should get up. I have to be at work in—" she twisted her neck to look at the clock "—less than an hour."

"No, you don't." Joe toyed with the ends of her hair. "Gorgeous George told you to stay home today."

"Unfortunately, George—Jim," she corrected herself crossly, "—didn't volunteer to cover my shift."

"He didn't. Your other friends did. Parker, Morales and Nguyen."

She narrowed her eyes. "I don't remember that."

"You got hit on the head. I'm surprised you remember anything."

He had a point.

She lay there, trying not to make a big deal out of

the fact that her breasts were squashed against his chest and he was still really aroused.

"So, I guess you still have to get up, huh?" she asked.

His eyes laughed at her. "I can't believe you would give me a straight line like that. I am up."

She shivered. Yes, he was. "I meant, to go to work."

"I'm not going anywhere," he said huskily.

She knew better.

An optimist in other ways, Nell had no illusions about how this scenario played out. The people she loved always left. At least, they always left her.

But Joe had cared enough to bring her home. To fix her soup. To spend the night. That was something.

And if he stayed even another hour... Her blood beat with the possibilities. That could be something else.

She moistened her lips, aware he watched the movement of her tongue.

Stretching a fraction of an inch, she touched her lips to his jaw. She feathered kisses to the side of his mouth, the rise of his cheekbone, the corner of his eye.

He threaded his fingers through her hair to hold her still. "Nell... Do you know what you're doing?"

Her nerves jumped. Bad question. If she thought about what she was doing, she might never have the guts to go through with it.

She had condoms in her bedside table. After two-and-a-half years, were they still any good?

Was she?

Nipping his chin, she fused her mouth to his until

he kissed her back, hard. Until his tongue pushed into her mouth and his hips thrust upward from the bed.

Triumphant, breathless, she pulled back and asked him, "What do you think?"

"I think you're killing me," he said, and reached for her again.

She crawled on top of him, which was awkward because the blankets were in the way, but he helped her, shoving, tugging until she straddled his body, nothing between them but their clothes. His jeans felt rough, exciting, against the soft inner skin of her thighs. His chest was hot and solid against her breasts. Her nipples tightened. She rubbed against him. He was hot and solid all over, and he kept on kissing her, his mouth warm and urgent, as his hands stroked up her sides and found her breasts through the thin cotton T-shirt she wore. He weighed them, shaped them, and she shivered because it felt so good, because he felt so good, thick and eager against her.

The ridge of his arousal pressed against her stomach. She squirmed to get a better fit between their bodies, pushing his hands aside when he tried again to help, struggling with his zipper and her panties on her own.

Finally he was free. She touched him. He was hot and hard, smooth and sleek, and hers. Hers for the taking.

She was panting, dizzy and dry mouthed with triumph and fear, as she covered him for her own protection, as she eased herself over him and onto him. She caught her breath.

Nell was a nurse. She saw male bodies all the time, examined them, diagnosed them, treated them, but always holding herself separate, never truly touching, never touched.

Joe touched her. He filled her, stretched her, steadied her, his breathing deep and slow, as she took him. She moved on him with exquisite slowness, his pleasure hers, his powerful male body hers, until his hands came down on her hips, and he gripped her and moved her to his own rhythm.

Her concentration skipped. She thought she could, if she wanted, hold herself aloof from him and from what their two bodies were making together. Only a little apart, a little in control, in possession of her senses and herself.

Her blood pounded in her head. He hadn't even taken off his shirt. Neither of them had. Maybe this wasn't such a good—

Joe rocked up, into her, making her gasp, making her clench on him and moan. She grabbed his shoulders as he worked her, deeper, faster, overtaking her pace, stealing her breath.

He was there, touching her, inside her, with her, and she was so damn tired of being good and in control and alone that she let herself be with him. Let herself go with him. Let herself go.

Her muscles tightened. Her mind blanked.

His fingers bit into her rear as he thrust up. Pleasure slammed into her, hard. Again. Her body shimmered and shuddered. She came apart, crying out, and collapsed on his chest. Dimly, she was aware of him moving, thrusting, convulsing under her.

She clutched his shoulders and turned her face into his neck, embarrassed because she'd made noise and hadn't shaved her legs in ages and grateful because she wasn't alone.

* * *

That was so good he almost didn't need a cigarette.

Joe stroked Nell's hair and stared at the ceiling, waiting for the bed to stop heaving and his heartbeat to return to normal. Wondering how soon he could get up and check his jacket pockets. He was pretty sure he'd smoked all three of his cigarettes yesterday, and he hadn't been home to restock.

But a guy needed something to hold on to after his world had tilted on its axis.

Nell exhaled softly against his neck. Briefly, he considered holding on to her, but it was too soon for that. He was still destroyed from the first time. He ran his hand down her back, over her shirt. Next time, he was going to get her naked. Next time...

He drifted, idly rubbing the warm, firm curve of her butt. Her smooth thighs still straddled his hips. Her warm, damp sex nestled against him. His own body stirred in response. Maybe it wasn't too soon?

It wouldn't take much to roll her over, to push his way back into her round, tight body, to feel her stretch and pulse around him as he banged her into the headboard...

No. Head-banging sex with a woman who had a concussion was probably a bad idea. In fact, any kind of sex was probably on the list of Things to Avoid.

Joe scowled at a crack in the ceiling, trying to ignore the temptation of Nell's full, soft breasts pressed against his side. At least it hadn't been all his idea.

Which had to be the lamest excuse since, "It was only one drink."

Maybe he hadn't been able to control his response to her, but he was responsible for his actions now.

He needed to get up. Get out. Before he forgot all

his good intentions and took advantage of her again. Before he took *her,* round, tight, wet…

Damn.

"Is there a drugstore around here?" he asked.

Nell raised her head from his shoulder. "What?"

"A drugstore. I figured I'd go grab a paper and some cigarettes," he said, trying for casual and instead sounding like the kind of creep who rolled off a woman and immediately started looking for the nearest exit.

Which, come to think of it, pretty much described him before Nell.

"Maybe pick up some bagels for breakfast," he added. There. That made it clear he was coming back.

She sat up, folding her long, smooth legs under her, crossing her arms over her breasts. Her really nice breasts. "I'd prefer it if you don't smoke in my apartment."

He rolled away from her before he changed his mind and pulled her under him. "Not a problem," he said, reaching for his shoes. There was an open box of condoms in her nightstand, almost full. "I'm quitting."

"Then why do you need cigarettes?"

Joe stared at the box, the open box, the box with the expiration date stamped on the side, and felt his stomach implode. "I don't."

It was okay. He breathed. The box was good for another seven months. They were safe.

But the scare made him think. What was he doing? Suppose he'd gotten her pregnant? He was living his life one day at a time. Nell was a woman who deserved hopes, house plans and dreams of babies. She didn't need a guy like him in her life.

And he didn't know what to do with a woman like her.

"I see," Nell said, in that tone of voice a woman used when she really meant she was blind and you were a moron.

Joe stood. "Look, I'm not doing a good job of explaining."

Nell pulled on her robe and tied it around her with short, jerky movements. "Have I asked you for an explanation?"

This was not going well.

He followed Nell across the room. "No, but you're entitled to one."

"Why?" She kept departing from his script. Her eyes were bright with tears or temper. God, he hoped it was temper.

"Well, because you…" He fumbled, which surprised him. He'd always been able to talk his way out of—or into—almost anything. He was an Irishman born with the gift of blarney, a reporter with a knack for words, a man who had his lines down pat, from "Let me buy you a drink" to "I'll call you."

He tried again. "Because we…"

"Were intimate?"

Stupid word. "Intimate" didn't begin to describe how great it had felt to stay with her, to sleep with her, to wake up with her sweet and hot beside him.

But he nodded, relieved they were getting somewhere. "Yeah."

"Don't worry about it. We weren't that intimate." She stalked to her dresser and pulled clean underwear from a drawer. "You never even took off your pants."

Temper, definitely. And hurt, which neither of them

deserved. She'd been hurt enough, and he was trying harder than he'd ever tried in his life to make this work.

He opened his arms, dropped them to his sides. "What do you want from me?"

She swallowed. "Honesty, for starters. If you want to go, go. You don't need to make up some stupid excuse about buying a newspaper."

Joe shook his head. "I'm not leaving. You need somebody to stay with you for twenty-four hours."

That didn't come out the way he meant it. It sounded like he was staying with her on doctor's orders instead of because he wanted to.

But it worked, because she gave him one of those long, cool looks of hers and said, "Yes, of course. Thank you. I'm going to shower now. You do what you want."

Victory, Joe thought as he watched her walk away. So why did he feel like such a loser?

Chapter 12

The trouble with getting what you asked for was that you were supposed to be satisfied.

Nell cranked off the hot water and reached for a towel. But she wasn't. Satisfied. Not by a long shot.

She squeezed the water from her hair, wincing at the pain in her scalp. She'd asked Joe to be honest with her. The least she could do was be honest with herself.

Physically, well... She looked in the mirror at her body, the body she tended and mostly ignored, the body that had been calling attention to itself all morning with aches and tugs and twinges, and took inventory. Her head still pounded. That was concussion. Her nipples stood at attention. That could be cold. Her lips were swollen, she had a string of red marks on each hip that would probably turn into bruises, and every muscle in her body felt grateful. That was Joe, Joe and most definitely Joe.

But emotionally…

Nell sighed and patted herself dry with the towel, gently because her skin was still sensitized. She couldn't blame Joe for her discontent. He'd done his best to meet her demands.

It wasn't his fault that, after a lifetime of settling for less than she wanted, she suddenly didn't want to settle anymore.

His dark, frustrated face swam between her and the mirror. *What do you want from me?*

Her heart squeezed. She wanted too much.

She went into her bedroom to finish dressing. Joe wasn't there. Even his shoes were gone from under her bed.

She could be adult about this. All she had to do was convince him she was fine, and he could go, his responsibilities discharged. Her hands trembled as she pulled on her jeans.

Even though the swelling had gone down, she didn't want to tug a sweater over her head. She was buttoning her blouse when she heard an unfamiliar ring. Not her phone and not her pager.

Someone must be calling Joe. His editor, his mother, his brother, a friend.

She wasn't interested. She certainly wasn't jealous.

She walked—slowly, to demonstrate her lack of interest— into the kitchen, where Joe was pouring a cup of coffee with one hand and holding his cell phone to his ear with the other.

''I appreciate the heads up,'' he said into the phone.

Nell removed another mug from the cupboard, grateful for a distraction to bridge the morning-after awkwardness.

Joe held up the pot and she nodded. He poured,

still speaking into his cell phone. "Will he give her another day?"

His mouth compressed. "Fine, I'll ask him myself."

She added milk to her cup, aware she was eavesdropping and uncertain what to do about it. It was her kitchen. It was her coffee.

"No, I'll be here." Joe slid the pot back into the coffeemaker with unnecessary force. "We both know she didn't have anything to do with it." Nell's heart thumped. A pause, while he paced. "Yeah. Yeah, okay. You, too."

Frowning, he disconnected the call.

Nell wrapped both hands around her mug and sipped, trying to rein in her nerves, her needs and her curiosity. "Who was that?"

"My brother."

She swallowed. Which brother? The firefighter or the cop? "Mike? Is he all right?"

"He's fine."

So what had his-brother-the-cop said to upset him? *We both know she didn't have anything to do with it.* A warning shiver ran up her spine.

Joe patted his empty breast pocket and scowled. Obviously he hadn't gone out for cigarettes yet. Or bagels.

"Should I offer to cook some eggs?" she asked.

Joe gave her a level look. "Are you offering?"

"I don't know. I don't know the rules."

"The rules." He grinned. "There are rules?"

She bit her lip to keep her smile in check. This wasn't funny. She was vulnerable. At a disadvantage. "You would know."

"Other than, 'don't leave the seat up,' I can't think of any."

Did he need her to spell it out? "I don't want you to feel obliged to stay for breakfast just because we…because I…I don't want you to feel obliged."

Joe reached out and tucked a strand of her hair behind her ear. "I'm not obliged. I am hungry." His thumb brushed her jaw, intimate as a kiss. "Where's your frying pan?"

It was hardly a declaration of devotion or commitment. But it left her breathless and nearly speechless all the same.

"Under the stove," she managed.

"Right." He turned from her and dug in the storage drawer for her mother's cast-iron skillet. "Why don't you get out the eggs? You got any bread that doesn't look like a sixth-grade science-fair exhibit?"

She watched him make himself at home in her kitchen, torn between pleasure at having him here and resentment that this was so easy for him.

"In the freezer," she said. "I don't go through a loaf very quickly on my own."

"Practical of you." He tossed a chunk of butter into the pan.

She wasn't sure that was a compliment. She would have liked to hear that she was beautiful or sexy or exciting. But she was practical, she thought, crossing to the refrigerator. Competent. She yanked open the freezer door. Self-sufficient.

She dropped two slices of bread into the toaster. "You understand you don't have to stay after breakfast."

"Yeah, I do." Joe swirled the pan to melt the last of the butter and set it back on the burner. "You've got a detective coming to talk to you this morning, and I want to be here.''

Nell almost dropped the carton of eggs. ''Why? I gave my statement to your brother last night.''

Joe took the eggs and broke them one by one into the pan. Crack, plop. ''Mike's going to follow up on that. This is something else.''

Misgiving shook her. ''What do you mean, something else? Did something happen at the clinic?''

All his attention focused on the eggs sizzling in the pan. ''Not exactly.''

''Then, what? Exactly.'' Apprehension sharpened her voice.

Joe shifted the pan to another burner and turned to face her. ''The investigation turned up a bunch more phony prescriptions written on clinic pads to clinic patients that the patients never received.''

Her mind struggled to grasp the implications of what he was saying. ''But if the prescriptions were never picked up—''

''The drugs were picked up,'' Joe said. ''But not by patients.''

Nell absorbed the news like a body blow. ''Then, who...?''

''That's what the police want to know. Somebody's making the pickups. The costs are charged to the patients or their insurance companies, and the drugs are resold on the street. The profits are probably split with whoever is providing the prescriptions.''

''Who is the prescriber?'' Nell whispered. But she knew. She knew.

''The prescriptions have your name on them,'' Joe said quietly. ''Your signature. The area sergeant assigned a detective to the case this morning, and they've notified the DEA.''

Nell went numb. This went beyond bad and into nightmare.

''How many prescriptions?''

How much damage had been done in her name? To her name?

''Mike wouldn't say.'' Joe's tone was flat.

Why not?

''Because you're a reporter?'' Nell asked.

Joe opened cupboard doors until he found her neatly stacked plates. ''That's part of it.''

She twisted her fingers together. ''Or because you're sleeping with me?''

Joe banged the cabinet shut. ''He doesn't know that.''

Her heart constricted. ''He knows you spent the night.''

''He also knows you're not guilty,'' Joe said. ''Or he would if he had half a brain. Sit down and eat your eggs.''

Her stomach churned. She couldn't possibly eat now. But she sank onto a chair. ''My name was on the prescriptions, you said. Your brother has to think I'm guilty. That's why he called, isn't it? He doesn't want you involved.''

Joe slid the eggs from the skillet onto two plates. ''That's because he's not looking at this objectively.''

She appreciated his logic, but his detachment hurt. ''And you are?''

''Sure. You're the one who reported a problem in the first place. You wouldn't have called the police if you were guilty.''

Her hands were cold. She was cold all over. "Unless I wanted to divert their suspicions."

Joe popped toast from the toaster. "Nope. This drug-fraud thing didn't surface until after Mike and Dietz showed up at your clinic the first time. My guess is whoever was stealing from the pharmacy figured they couldn't get away with it anymore and came up with this scheme instead."

"But prescription fraud is a much bigger deal. Bigger risks and bigger penalties."

Joe shrugged and set both plates on the table. "It also has a bigger payoff. Your crooks could be desperate. Or greedy."

"Or convinced they can pin it on me."

"That's why I want to be here when you talk to the detective."

The temptation to say yes staggered her. It would be too easy to go along with him, to simply give up control of her fate and the situation.

She cleared her throat. "That might not be such a good idea."

Joe stabbed his eggs. "Why not?"

"Well, for starters, I don't think the detective will let you. You're not my lawyer. And as much as I appreciate your being here last night—"

"And this morning," Joe put in blandly. "Don't forget this morning."

Her face got hot. The heat moved low inside her, too, her own personal lava flow. She couldn't forget this morning if she tried.

Nell took a deep breath. "As much as I appreciate what you've done—everything you've done—I don't need a nurse, either."

Joe grinned. "Babe, you don't know what you need."

But she did.

She'd had the past two years and all morning to figure it out.

She played with her toast. "Maybe I should say, I know what I don't need."

His grin faded. "And that would include me."

She couldn't afford to need him. Didn't he see?

"It's really nice of you to offer," she said earnestly, and winced.

Nice. God, that sounded so lame.

He lowered his knife and fork. "Is this because I'm a reporter?" he asked abruptly.

She blinked. "What?"

A muscle worked in his jaw. "Because I get it, you know. I can do 'off the record.'"

He was angry, which she expected.

And hurt, which she did not. She didn't want to hurt him. She only wanted to protect herself.

She shook her head—another mistake, it made her dizzy—and assured him, "It's not that."

"Then what the hell is it? Because I don't have a clue."

"It's just…" She struggled for an explanation that would satisfy him. "I'm innocent. I'll be fine."

He looked at her as if she had the word "stupid" emblazoned on her forehead. Maybe she did.

"You were innocent before, and you still got dumped and screwed."

She forced a smile, trying to keep her tone light. Trying to keep their disagreement from getting too close. Too real. "Well, I've been screwed again, and it wasn't nearly as bad as I remember."

"'Not as bad'? Wow. Thanks. That's one I'll have them carve on my tombstone."

There was a hollow in her chest and a buzzing in her head. She leaned forward and covered one of his hands, his beautiful surgeon's hands, with her own. "Joe, this is not about you."

"No, it's about you. About how you can't accept help."

She didn't want him to see that. She should have realized his sharp reporter's eyes saw everything. "Maybe."

His mouth tightened. "Or is it just that you can't accept help from me?"

She drew back her hand. "You know that I like you." Oh, now there was an understatement. She tried again. "That I care for you."

"But you don't trust me not to let you down. You don't count on me to be there for you when you have a problem."

She couldn't count on anyone. She'd taught herself not to rely on anyone. Because when you did and they betrayed and abandoned you, you not only had the wreckage of your life to pick up but the pieces of your heart.

She hid her trembling hands in her lap and tried to keep her voice from shaking. "I thought you'd appreciate me not making any demands on you. You're an observer. You write about other people's lives, about other people's problems. You don't do involved. I don't expect you to."

"News flash for you, babe. We had sex this morning. That makes us involved in my book."

That jerked her chin up. "I don't think so. You

told your mother we were having a torrid, temporary affair.''

His eyes were like ice chips. ''Is that what you want?''

This wasn't about what she wanted, either. It was about what life had taught her she could have.

Her head throbbed. Wrapping her hands around her coffee mug, she raised her gaze to his. ''Are you offering me an alternative? After one night together?''

He jolted as if she'd just shocked him with an electric paddle. So she had her answer. It was her own fault if she didn't like it.

''I'm offering to stay,'' Joe said, suddenly cautious. ''I'm offering to help.''

It was more than anyone else was prepared to do. More, Nell guessed, than Joe in his nomadic, footloose life was used to giving.

It was almost enough.

But she couldn't put herself in the position of relying on another person ever again.

''I don't want you to think I'm ungrateful. But I'd really prefer to handle this myself.''

His chair scraped the floor as he stood. He paced to the sink and turned, glowering at her.

Already moving away. Moving on.

''I don't like leaving you alone like this.''

She had always been alone, even when she was married. At least now she recognized it.

Nell sipped her coffee, but it didn't do anything for the pounding in her head or the churning in her stomach. Or the tears that brewed behind her eyes and in her throat.

''I'll call Billie,'' she said, to make it easier for

him to go. "I'm sure she'll come over at the end of her shift to check on me."

He drained his mug and set it in the sink, and one stupid corner of her brain still thought he would ignore her urging and her logic and stay. They scraped her plates and stacked her dishwasher together, and one stubborn corner of her heart still hoped he'd reject the exit she was offering.

"I wrote my cell number by the phone," he told her as she stood in the hall, waiting for him to leave so she could have a good cry. "Call if you need anything."

She needed him.

But pride and self-preservation kept her silent. And he left without her saying a word.

He should have said something.

Joe slammed the Range Rover's door. The sound echoed between the rows of cars in the parking lot.

Yeah, like anything he said could have changed Nell's mind.

He stomped toward the church hall, where the seven o'clock meeting was already underway in the basement. He so didn't need this. He was tired. He'd worked late filing the first story in his series on Chicago's uninsured. Right now he didn't want to get blind and stupid drunk so much as he wanted to go bang on Nell's apartment door or howl under her window.

But he knew the triggers: anger, pain, frustration, depression, stress, anxiety. Check, check, check… He was working his way through the list and that meant, like it or not, need it or not, convenient or not, he was due for a meeting.

He slipped through a door at the back of a room that smelled of floor polish and bad coffee. A tough young Hispanic was talking and gesturing at the front. An elderly woman in a neat navy suit was sitting directly beside him, nodding her head in time to the movement of his hands.

It was a closed discussion meeting tonight. Joe chose a chair near the back and let the stories wash over him, halting admissions of pain and purpose, haunting confessions of despair and hope.

"Hi, my name is Carmen…"

"Rick…"

"Kathleen…"

"Joe…"

"…and I'm an alcoholic."

He didn't know all the names, but he was one of them. One with them. Gradually, the stories and support seeped through his distraction. Slowly, his frustration drained away, and peace trickled in to take its place.

Maybe he'd needed this more than he thought.

At the end, Joe stood to pour himself some of the lousy coffee and exchange greetings.

"Hi." A female voice. Young.

He turned.

Bright blue eyelids, long brown hair, kid in a stroller. The woman looked vaguely familiar. He'd never seen the kid before in his life.

"Do you come here a lot?" the young woman asked, and then rolled her eyes. "Jeez. I can't believe I said that. Classic pickup line, huh?"

Joe smiled at her reassuringly. "I'm so out of the bar scene, it sounded new to me."

She smiled back, her face relaxing. "Joe, right? I've seen you at the clinic."

He recognized her now. "Melody King. You work there," he said.

They shook hands, a ritual complicated by his coffee cup, her slipping purse, her dangling umbrella and the stroller.

Nell's office manager was an alcoholic?

Joe's gaze dropped to the little girl kicking pink shoes against the stroller's footrest. "And who is this?"

"That's my Rosie." The young mother stooped to unfasten the child's seat restraint and lift her in her arms. "She's getting too big for the stroller, but it keeps her quiet during the meetings. At least, it keeps her from running around."

Was it just booze? Joe wondered. Or booze and drugs? Was she relapsed or recovering? Did Nell know?

He had to say something.

"Does she usually come with you?"

"No, I have a sitter." Melody shifted her daughter on her hip. "But she canceled, and I really needed to come tonight, you know?"

He knew.

"So I brought her here with me. A lot of the folks in this group, they're kind of old, but they mostly don't mind."

"That's good," Joe said.

He was not going to ask, he decided. The purpose of the meeting was mutual support and recovery. He was not going to violate the bond of the group by interrogating Melody King in the church basement.

"Of course, I've been coming so long, some of

them know me from when I was pregnant.'' Melody pushed back her curtain of hair with one hand and peered up at Joe. Apparently she took seriously the organization's tradition of making strangers welcome. ''So, you're like, new, right?''

''This is my second time here,'' Joe admitted. ''I usually go to the Halstead Street group.''

She nodded. ''Oh, yeah. I guess that's closer to where you work, huh? Hang on, baby,'' she crooned to her squirming daughter. ''She gets kind of restless after eight o'clock,'' she confided to Joe. ''We probably should get going.''

Still balancing the child on her hip, she struggled to turn the stroller. A wheel bumped the coffee table.

Joe caught a stack of foam cups before they toppled. ''Let me give you a hand to your car.''

''I don't have a car.''

It was only a little overcast. She probably enjoyed her walk home. He had no reason to…

Nell's comment ran through his mind, jagged and clear as a crack in the sidewalk. *You're an observer. You don't do involved. I don't expect you to.*

Hell.

''Can I give you a lift?'' he asked. ''You probably don't accept rides from strangers, but—''

''That would be great,'' Melody said. ''Besides, you're not really a stranger. I mean, you came to the meeting. That's got to count for something. And you're seeing Nell, and I figure she wouldn't go with you if there was, like, something wrong with you, you know?''

Joe dragged the stroller to one side and pushed open the door. Swell. Even the office manager acknowledged his bond with Nell. Why the hell couldn't she?

Melody scooted past him, still holding the kid. "Unless you're one of her lame ducks," she said over her shoulder.

He carried the stroller up from the basement, aware of his ankle grinding with every step. "Lame duck?"

"Oh, you know," Melody said at the top of the stairs. "People like me. People who need help. She collects them."

Disquiet prodded him. He didn't want to be part of a collection. "Give me an example."

"Well…me. Nobody else would hire me. I've got the single-mom thing going, and I'm a former crack-head."

He hadn't asked her. But now that she'd volunteered the information, Joe didn't know whether to be glad or sorry.

"Besides you," he said, and opened the door to the parking lot.

A fine rain glowed around the streetlights and gleamed on the cars.

"Ooh, I'm glad you're driving," Melody said.

"Do you want me to bring the car around?"

"No, I'm good," Melody said. "Hand me Rose's sweater, though, would you?"

He fished in the stroller until he found it, a fuzzy pink thing with a hood. He handed it to her. "So, who else at the clinic owes Nell?"

"Well, she has her special pet patients. People nobody else wants to see. Mrs. Delaggio—what a bitch—and that grumpy old Mr. Vacek. And then there's Ed Johnson. I know he had to retire from his last job. He doesn't like what he's making at the clinic, but without Nell he wouldn't have a job at all.''

Interesting. But was the elderly pharmacist broke enough or resentful enough to target the woman who had hired him?

"What about Lucy Morales? Or Billie Parker?"

Melody kneeled with her daughter and began to coax her chubby arms into the sweater's sleeves. "Lucy's first husband liked to pound on her, and Billie helps support her sister and her little boy.''

"But they both could get jobs somewhere else, right? They don't have records or anything.''

Melody adjusted the hood over Rose's curls. "Aren't you cute?''

Joe started. She was talking to the kid. Wasn't she?

Melody stood with Rose on her hip. "Lucy used to run with the Conquistas. She showed me her tattoo once. But I don't think she was ever arrested.''

The Conquistas were a girl gang. Joe couldn't remember if they were into drugs or not. Mike would know.

They hurried through the rain, Melody burdened by her daughter, Joe hampered by the stroller and his ankle.

"This is mine,'' he said, stopping beside the Range Rover.

"Nice,'' approved Melody. "Do you have a car seat?''

The rain dripped down. Joe stared at her blankly. He'd never thought of that.

"Guess not,'' Melody said. "Oh, well. Thanks for the offer.''

The wind blew, and the rain came down harder, colder, than before.

Joe unlocked the SUV's doors. "Get in the back. I'll go slow."

"I don't know…"

He grabbed the stroller and stowed it in the trunk. Melody ducked into the back seat as rain pelted the roof.

"All set?" Joe asked, bending to look in on them.

Melody tightened her daughter's seat belt. "I guess. You don't have any kids, do you?"

A year—six months—two weeks ago, he would have shuddered at the thought. Anyone he worked with would have laughed.

"Do I look like I have kids?"

"Well, I don't know," Melody said, settling comfortably against the black leather seat and putting an arm around her daughter. "You're the right age."

She meant old.

Joe closed the rear door with an audible snap and got behind the wheel.

"Just for the record," he said to the rearview mirror, "I do not have kids."

Melody nodded, undeterred. "Ever married?"

"No." That sounded too bald. Defensive. "In my job, I travel a lot. At least, I used to."

"That's probably why you can afford such a nice car." With a little sigh, the office manager leaned back against the head rest. "Jim—Dr. Fletcher—drives a Subaru."

Joe's wiper blades beat against the rain. "I thought doctors all drove Mercedes."

"His first wife drives the Mercedes. His second wife drives a Porsche."

"Tough on a guy," Joe said dryly.

Melody straightened. "Turn right up there. Fourth

building on the left. And it is tough,'' she said. ''He can't afford to have any kind of relationship now, you know?''

Joe turned the corner, wondering how much Fletcher had exaggerated his financial hardships to keep the starry-eyed office manager at bay.

Unless he hadn't.

Unless Dr. Kildare really was strapped for cash. In which case, the ex-wives weren't an excuse. They could be a motive.

Joe double-parked in front of Melody's dilapidated apartment block. What if the doctor was supplementing his income with a little judicious prescription fraud?

And what if Joe only wanted the guy to be guilty because he was sober, successful and whole?

Nell didn't like doctors, he reminded himself as he unloaded the stroller from the back and limped up the walk in the rain. She liked him. She'd had sex with him. That proved it. A woman like Nell didn't crawl on top of a man unless there was something between them. Lust, yeah, sure, but liking, too. Affection. Respect. Trust.

Joe thought of Nell's determination to handle everything on her own, and his gut tightened.

Unless he was another one of her ducks. Not just lame, but crippled.

Chapter 13

Billie crossed her arms in the doorway to Nell's office. "If I'd had thirty-six hours to play house with Joe Reilly, I'd be smiling."

Nell looked up from the stacks of paper spawned by her absence. She didn't feel like smiling.

"We didn't play house," she said, dismissing the memories of Joe, heating her soup. Joe, pouring her coffee. Joe, hot and hard under her and inside her, straining together as the light streaked beneath her window shade. "He took me home, he made sure I was okay, and he left before you and Detective Ward came over."

Billie raised her eyebrows. "And he never came back to tuck you into bed?"

Nell moved a stack of glossy drug-company brochures to a corner of her desk. "Nope."

"No?"

"No." Nell bit out the word. "I told him to leave, and he left."

Billie shook her head. She'd bleached her hair again, short, fuzzy, dandelion yellow. "Honey, that concussion scrambled your brain. You don't send a man like that packing."

Nell's temples throbbed, her scalp ached and there was a too familiar emptiness around her heart. Maybe her friend was right. But admitting it didn't help at all.

"Billie, we're in the middle of a felony investigation. Detective Ward took over my office this morning to question my staff. I'm behind on my paperwork, and my afternoon appointments start in five minutes. This is a really bad time for me to be thinking of starting anything with anybody. Even Joe Reilly."

Especially Joe Reilly, who made her feel…too much.

Billie sniffed. "Fine. But before you blow the man off entirely, you might take a look at the paper."

"I've seen the paper," Nell said wearily. "That article's been plastered up by the flow board for over a week."

"'Delivering Hope'? That was pretty sweet."

It was more than sweet, Nell thought. It was proof Joe was not the burned-out cynic he made himself out to be. His idealism might be tarnished, but his values shone in every word he wrote.

I'm offering to stay, he'd said, his blue eyes wary. *I'm offering to help.*

It wasn't his fault she wanted more.

"But I meant today's paper," Billie continued.

"What are you talking about?"

"The article in the paper. Front page. Didn't you see it?"

Nell shook her head dumbly.

"Melody brought it in. I didn't read the whole thing. There was a bunch about unemployment benefits and medical insurance and I don't know what all. But there was a lot about the clinic patients and a real nice bit on you. That's why I thought you two might be, like, involved."

Nell was nearly breathless with hope and distress. He'd written about her in the paper?

"He probably just needed a hook for his story," she said, getting up from her desk.

Billie shrugged. "Whatever. He sure made us look good, though. Bet we see some more donations."

Nell clutched the stethoscope around her neck.

"Hey, I thought you'd be happy," Billie said.

"I am. It's just..."

He'd never told her. Oh, she knew Joe's editor had asked him to write a series on health insurance. But he hadn't told her he was writing about her. He hadn't told her he'd made it back on the front page. They'd swapped body fluids, but he hadn't shared a bit of himself.

And yet he'd given her exactly the kind of media attention she wanted and her bottom line needed.

Her stomach churned. Her head throbbed.

Billie frowned. "Are you all right?"

"Fine," Nell said brightly. "Never better."

She grabbed her clipboard and went in search of her two o'clock appointment.

Maybe if she kept moving, she wouldn't notice she wasn't getting anywhere.

* * *

"Congratulations," Nell greeted Joe when he opened his front door. "You made page one."

He squinted at her, confused, and so damn glad to see her that for about five seconds or so he could overlook the strain behind her smile and the shadows that lay like bruises under her eyes. He bet she'd put in a full day at work, damn it. She should be home in bed.

Nell in bed. Great idea. Bad move.

He shoved his hands in his pockets to keep from grabbing her and demanded, "What are you doing here? You look like hell."

Her bright smile slipped. She glared back at him. "So I'll never get asked to do a testimonial for Cover Girl. Are you going to invite me in?"

He stepped back to admit her over the threshold. She must have come directly from the clinic. She was wearing the neat slacks and tidy blouse he thought of as her uniform, and in her hands she carried...

"What's in the bag?"

"I brought dinner." She held it up for his inspection. "To celebrate your return to the front page."

He eyed her warily. Dinner, fine. But something wasn't right. Her shoulders were stiff beneath her martial red cloak, and her tone was warm and false as hell.

"Below the fold," he pointed out. "On a slow news day."

"Still, you must be pleased."

He took the bag from her and headed back to the kitchen. "Actually, I hoped you would be pleased."

"With the publicity? I am. It's wonderful. Thank you," she said, the way you thanked the dentist after a root canal.

Joe's mouth quirked. So much for his little fantasy in which Nell, overcome with gratitude, begged him to spend the night with her. The whole night, and none of this thanks-for-sex-and-I-can-handle-the-rest-myself stuff the next morning, either.

He put on the kettle for tea. "Did you read it?" he asked.

"Of course. It's very good."

She was here. She was saying all the right things. So why did he feel cheated?

"Did you see the quote?"

He'd quoted her, right after his demographic break-down on the percentage of the city's population that didn't have health insurance.

"It's not about statistics," said Eleanor Dolan, director of the Ark Street Free Clinic. The clinic provides both quality medical care and a sense of dignity to those it serves. "My patients aren't numbers. They're people."

Nell nodded, perching on a bar stool pulled up to the island. Joe liked his kitchen, a big, old-fashioned room with oak cabinets and a hardwood floor. He wondered if Nell noticed. And why he cared.

"I never expected that remark to make the front page of the paper," she said.

"It was a great line."

Her gaze slid sideways. "Is that why you used it?"

"I used it because I thought it would do the clinic some good." He dropped two tea bags into mugs. "I figured it might do you some good, too."

"We got a nice bump in donations from your article about the Massouds."

"You'll see more this time," he promised. "A couple of checks already came in, in care of the paper. Somebody even dropped off a huge wad of cash in an envelope. My editor was impressed."

"I am, too."

"Money is good. Especially if it's a gauge of your public support."

At last he'd shaken her polite, bright facade. "Is that why you did it? To support me?"

He shrugged. "Can't hurt to let that detective see who he's dealing with."

"Joe." Her eyes were troubled. "This isn't your fight."

His gut hollowed. She couldn't have made it more clear that she didn't need him. That she didn't want him.

"It's my job," he persisted stubbornly, "to write the truth."

She blinked at him. She still didn't get it.

The kettle whistled. He lowered the heat under it and turned to face her.

"I didn't do you any favors," Joe said. "I write what I see. And what I see when I look at you is hope. Commitment. Compassion. I watch the way you take responsibility for everyone and everything around you, and I can see that you care. You care for the losers and the lame ducks and the people who need a second chance or who never had that much of a shot to begin with. You care so much, you even make me care. Which kind of pisses me off, but there it is."

She reached across the island and touched his arm. "Joe…"

"Let me finish." He took a breath, trying not to

be distracted by her touch. "So if you don't like me getting involved, tough. Get over it. Just because your ex was a creep and you're working with a crook does not mean you have to lie down for the investigating detective."

"Okay," Nell said. She was smiling.

"That's it? 'Okay'?"

She nodded.

"Why?" he demanded. "I mean, I don't want to screw myself over here, Dolan, but that was not me at my most charming and persuasive."

"That was why," Nell said simply. "I don't think you'd be that rude if you weren't sincere."

Her perception made him squirm. But she was right. She did challenge his detachment. She blew his cool. Being around her made it difficult to play his usual glib, defensive self. Which meant he had years of being tongue-tied and inarticulate to look forward to.

The thought didn't bother him nearly as much as it should have.

Joe believed in her.

He believed her.

Nell hugged her new knowledge to herself as they sat on his standard bachelor-issue, black leather couch and ate Chinese food out of cartons. Her legs were curled under her. His ankle was propped on the coffee table.

Her dinner ploy had worked. She was in charge of her own destiny, in control of the situation.

"Is there any garlic shrimp left?" she asked.

"Sure. Pass me the sesame beef."

They swapped little white boxes, and in that moment Nell was almost completely happy.

So what if Joe hadn't made a private declaration of love? A public declaration of faith was equally moving and almost as good. She would settle for that.

He dug into the carton with his chopsticks. She noticed he handled them easily, even the cheap disposable kind the restaurant had packed in with their order.

Joe Reilly, man of the world. The thought impressed and depressed her at the same time.

"So, how did your interview with Detective Ken go?" he asked.

Nell swallowed. "His name is Kevin. Kevin Ward."

"He looks like a Ken doll."

She smiled. He did: slick suit, stiff hair, plastic smile. "Well…" She sobered, remembering the detective's pointed questions and obvious disbelief. "He hasn't arrested me yet."

Joe's chopsticks lifted. "Is he planning to?"

"He'd like to. I think the only thing stopping him is the fact that none of the pharmacists who filled the prescriptions could identify my photo. In fact, two of them insisted the drugs were picked up by a black male in his late twenties or early thirties. So even though my name is on the prescriptions, there's nothing connecting me with the drugs on the other end."

Joe nodded. "Ward needs to find the money."

"I don't have any money."

"Not in the bank, maybe. But drug deals are cash transactions. Ward's going to look for any discrepancies in your cash flow. Unusual windfalls? Big purchases? Expensive habits?"

She thought. "I don't have anything like that."

"Who does?"

"Excuse me?"

"Somebody—probably somebody you work with, since whoever it is had access to your prescription pad and the clinic patient list—is profiting from the sale of those drugs on the street. I don't know the scope of the diversion, but if Mike is right and they've notified the DEA, they're going to expect big money somewhere."

"It hasn't been going on that long," Nell protested.

"Then think. Who needs money now? Or has money all of a sudden?"

Her contentment leaked away like the brown sauce in the bottom of the carton. "I don't want to talk about it. I haven't even let myself think about it much."

"You have to have some ideas."

"All right, yes, I do," she said, irritated with him for making her admit it. It felt like a betrayal, a shift in alliances, her-and-Joe when it had been her-and-the-clinic, and she wasn't ready for it. "That doesn't mean I have to act on them."

"Not admitting the problem doesn't make it go away," Joe said quietly.

Nell knew that. She had experience of that with Richard. And she resented Joe for pointing it out.

"You're not doing this person any favors by keeping quiet," he said.

"I don't know anything," she insisted.

"But you suspect."

Doubt and indecision ripped at her. "I don't know," she repeated. "I can't function if I go around suspecting everyone."

"You can't function if you're arrested, either. Who do you think might have done it?"

Nell set her open carton of shrimp on the coffee table. She wasn't hungry anymore.

"You have a responsibility here," Joe said. "A legal, moral responsibility to report someone you suspect of diverting drugs."

"I have a responsibility to the people who work with me, too," Nell said. "What if this person isn't doing it for the money?"

"You mean, stealing for personal use?"

She nodded, eager to convince him. Desperate to convince herself. "What if—this person—needs counseling? Treatment. Siccing the law on him might be the worst thing I could do. He might never recover."

"Ignore he has a problem, and I can guarantee he won't recover."

With her mind, Nell accepted what Joe was saying. But her heart panicked and retreated from the precipice he was leading her to.

"I don't want to go to the police," she blurted.

"We could go together."

She shook her head.

"You need to confront this guy with his problem. If nothing else, give him a chance to defend himself."

The chasm yawned wider at her feet. Her head pounded. Her throat ached. "I don't know if I can."

"Sure you can," said Joe. His tone was easy, but his gaze was sharp on her face. "You don't back down from anything."

"I did before." To her horror, she felt tears well in her eyes. "I never confronted Richard when I first thought he might be using drugs. It was my fault he didn't get the help he needed.''

"Bull," Joe said.

"It's true." She was flailing, falling into a deep, dark hole of responsibility and guilt. "I failed him, and I failed our marriage."

"You kept him from hitting bottom," Joe said. "And, yeah, maybe that was a mistake. Protecting an addict from the consequences of his addiction isn't going to motivate him to change. But that desire to change has to come from inside him. The choice to change is his. You don't have control over that any more than you have the power to cure the addiction."

"Then why should I try to do anything now? I couldn't even help my own husband."

"You don't need me to answer that," Joe said gently. "You're the one who told me if nobody cares, nothing gets done and nothing ever gets better."

"And you said you didn't believe that."

"Maybe I didn't. Maybe I forgot." He stretched his arm along the back of the couch, his hand brushing her shoulder. His fingers touched the ends of her hair. "Maybe I needed you to remind me."

"Damn it, Reilly." Her tears spilled over in defeat. "What do you want me to do?"

"You don't have to do anything on your own," he said. "Tell me who you think it is, and we'll figure it out from there."

You don't have to do anything on your own? Who was he kidding? Everything she'd ever accomplished in her life she'd done on her own.

Yeah, and look where that had gotten her.

She had a choice, she had a chance here, to do something differently.

If she trusted him.

She took a deep breath and, staring at the coffee table, said, "I'm afraid it's Melody."

He didn't say anything. Talk about your anticlimax.

Nell tried again. "Melody King? Our office manager. She—"

"I know who Melody is. I don't think she did it."

O-kay.

"The thing is, she knows where the pads are. And the patient lists. I know what you're going to say," Nell added, because she didn't, really, and he was sitting so strangely still. "Any staffer at the clinic could find or make an opportunity to steal a prescription pad. But Melody is the only one who has a drug habit. Had a drug habit."

"Do you have any reason to think she's using again?"

"I don't have any proof. But I can't prove she isn't using, either. It's not like she reports to me every time she goes to an AA meeting."

Joe turned his head and looked at her, and her heart lurched a little, because his mouth was so grim and his jaw was so tight. Without even knowing what was wrong, she ached for him.

"She goes to her meetings," he said.

Nell closed her mouth and tried to breathe normally. "How would you know?" she whispered.

"Because I've seen her there." His voice was flat. Detached. His eyes were miserable. "I'm an alcoholic, Nell. A narcotics addict. Just like your ex-husband."

Chapter 14

Nell stared at him, stunned, like the victim of a bar fight. Like he'd just cracked a bottle over her head.

"Why are you telling me this?"

Joe felt lousy. He deserved to feel lousy. He'd known he would feel lousy, and he'd opened his big mouth anyway.

"Melody's a good kid," he said. "I think you should trust her."

"Even if it means saying something you know will make me distrust you?"

He winced. Well, what did he expect? *Oh, darling, I love you so much, I don't care what you've done?* Fat chance.

He was a victim of his writer's imagination. He was concocting castles in the air, never-gonna-happen scenarios of Nell on his couch, in his bed, in his life…

She was still watching him, still waiting for his reply.

He grunted. "Yeah."

"So you would rather I blame you for something you did do than suspect her for something she didn't." Nell's voice was cool, her wording precise.

He eyed her warily. Where was she going with this?

"That's what I said."

She nodded, as if he'd confirmed something she had known all along.

"And you go to the meetings? AA?"

"Yeah. I told you, I saw Melody there."

"Then you are nothing at all like my ex-husband," Nell said.

He started breathing again. Hoping. Wishing.

Total mistake.

Because the next words out of her mouth were, "Are you still using?"

"No." He didn't take offense at her question. She deserved to know. And it was one answer he could give her that he wasn't ashamed of.

"How long have you been…" She hesitated.

"In recovery? Seven months."

Two hundred and fourteen days, each and every one of them a victory.

"And before that?"

"How long was I an alcoholic junkie, do you mean?"

She flushed. He'd flustered her. "No, I… Well, um…" She met his gaze, and her mouth firmed. "Yes."

"I can't quantify it for you as exactly. I probably always drank too much. Reporters in a war zone, trapped in bad hotels at night, trying to out-

Hemingway each other? We all drank. But I was holding it together, or thought I was, until Iraq.''

"What happened in Iraq?" she asked quietly.

Joe pulled his leg down from the coffee table. He wasn't used to being on this side of an interview. "It's a long story."

"I'm a good listener."

Yeah, she was.

Joe stared at his hands, clasped together between his knees. "You have to understand I was really pumped just to be there. We all were. We were embedded with the troops, invaders or liberators, it didn't matter. There was so much testosterone swirling around the press corps you would have taken us for a sandstorm. We had unprecedented access to report on the action, and yet all the information was spun just enough to make every one of us determined to get the angle, the insight, the shot that would tell the folks back home what it was really like over there."

"You won an award, your brother said. For your piece on the looting of Baghdad."

"Yeah, I won an award. Although by the time they gave it to me, I can't say I really cared."

"Because you were injured."

He'd like her to think that.

Joe had spoken in the past to his sponsor, to his priest and to other addicts in recovery. But he had never taken Step Five outside the safe circle of AA, never talked about his experience to his colleagues or his family.

Admitted to God, to ourselves and to another human being the exact nature of our wrongs.

"I didn't care because at the awards ceremony I was doped out of my mind," he corrected harshly.

It was no satisfaction at all to see Nell flinch.

Doggedly, Joe continued.

"The day I broke my ankle, going after that story... I wouldn't quit. Adrenaline, I guess. Or pride. Or sheer stupidity. I laced that sucker really tight and took pills for the pain and kept on reporting. When that didn't work anymore, I convinced the medics to slap on a walking cast and give me stronger pills. Compared to what I saw going on around me, the suffering, it didn't seem like that big a deal."

Joe exhaled. "Only I wasn't healing. And in a week or two, what had been a simple fracture was hamburger meat shot through with bone and held together from the outside. By then I was taking anything I could beg or find to get me through, narcotics for the pain and diet pills to kick me up enough to get out in the morning and booze to settle me down to sleep at night."

Beside him, Nell stirred.

She'd probably heard enough excuses from her ex to last a lifetime. She didn't need to hear more from him.

"I told you it was a long story," he said.

But she leaned forward and put her hand on his knee, a nurse's touch, warm and impersonal. He supposed he should be grateful she was willing to touch him at all.

"Go on."

"There's not much more to tell."

And not much she would believe. People with drug and alcohol problems were notorious liars. They lied to themselves. They lied to their bosses and co-workers. They lied to the people who loved them.

"You came back to the States," Nell prompted.

"I crashed, and the paper brought me home." He went as quickly and lightly as he could, as if that would keep him from sinking. "I was admitted to the hospital for surgery, which didn't help my ankle or my drug problem. And after three months of feeling sorry for myself and making my family miserable, I figured out my life was a mess and my career was a wash and I needed help to get sober."

He risked a look at her, hoping he didn't sound as pathetic as he felt.

Her clear blue eyes gazed back, all that practical intelligence and soft compassion focused on him. His stomach twisted in anxiety.

"That's why you never drink," Nell said.

He figured she'd notice that.

"Yeah."

"And why you won't get the surgery you need on your ankle."

Whoa. He hadn't expected her to make that connection.

"Yeah." He cleared his aching throat. "Pretty lame, huh?"

"I think it's remarkably disciplined," Nell said in her brisk, no-nonsense way. When he gaped at her, she added, "And also very brave. But are you sure it's necessary? There are nonnarcotic analgesics which—"

Joe recovered enough to interrupt her. "I won't take that chance."

Great. Like pathetic and lame weren't bad enough. He had to expose himself as a pathetic, lame coward.

"You should consider it," Nell said gently. "You have to think about your future."

"No, I don't. I can't. I'm living my life one day at a time now."

That was what AA taught you. To stay sober, one day at a time.

Nell watched him, her eyes troubled and her mouth tragic.

Regret lanced his heart.

He grinned at her, deliberately lightening the atmosphere between them. "I've got to work on my moves. A beautiful woman shows up on my doorstep with Chinese and congrats, and I top off the evening playing Truth or Dare."

He was relieved when she smiled back. "It does spoil the mood a little," she admitted.

There was the understatement of the year.

Joe got awkwardly to his feet. "Come on. I'll take you home."

Nell stayed where she was. "Unless the woman particularly admired honesty."

His heart slammed into his ribs.

She lifted her chin. "Unless she respected you for trying to protect someone else."

Unfolding her long legs from under her, she stood close enough to bring his body to sudden, tingling attention. She rested her palms lightly against his chest. Her hair brushed his jaw. He could smell her shampoo.

"Maybe we both should try to take things one day at a time," she said.

He gulped in air, certain he had misunderstood her. Praying he had not.

"What things?" he asked hoarsely.

"This." She stood on tiptoe to touch her lips to his. "Us."

They were an "us"? Hot damn.

But taking him on, his past, his problems, was an enormous risk. A step in the dark for a woman who liked to see her way. A leap of faith for a woman whose trust had been battered and betrayed. As much as Joe wanted her, he couldn't let her jump into this with her eyes closed.

"Are you sure?"

"No," Nell admitted with devastating honesty. "But I want to be. Why don't you try to convince me?"

His blood drummed in his head. "I don't want to talk you into anything you're not ready for."

She smiled. "So don't talk," she suggested.

That would work. She'd robbed him of speech anyway.

He spread his hands low over her round rear end and tugged her closer. He liked the way she fit against him, her strong bones and wide hips and soft breasts. He kissed her slowly, taking his time, enjoying the warmth of her body and the spicy heat of her mouth.

Convince me.

He took a sharp breath and moved his hands up, cupping the undersides of her breasts, brushing his thumbs over her nipples. They formed tight points beneath her shirt. He rubbed them through the fabric and then reached for the buttons on her blouse.

Her hands closed over his. "Where is your bedroom?"

He glanced over her shoulder at his wide, uncurtained living-room windows. "Down the hall."

Hand in hand, they crossed his foyer—he was relieved when she didn't bolt for the door—to his room. Nell paused inside, her gaze traveling over the furniture he'd inherited from his grandmother, the icon from Kosovo, the art glass from Israel, the red-and-black kilim on his bed.

"Wow. I was kind of expecting black satin sheets and a water bed."

He leaned against the door frame. "Disappointed?"

"No, this is better." She turned and slid her arms around his waist, smiling up at him, making him dizzy. "More you."

"I can give you more me," he promised, and kissed her again.

This time she let him unbutton her blouse. Underneath she was all smooth curves and soft cotton. His breath hissed in appreciation. She pushed the shirt from his shoulders. They undressed each other, taking time to kiss, to touch, pausing to praise and admire.

Convince me.

He pulled her tight against him, making her feel his hot arousal, stroking her back, caressing the cool curves of her rear end. She was beautiful. Naked. His.

He grabbed a condom from the bathroom, leaving the light on over the sink, and then walked Nell backward until her legs bumped the side of his mattress. He pressed her down until her pale hair spread against the red tapestry of his bed. She watched him quietly, her eyes unshuttered, her lips curved. He laced his fingers with hers and slid home.

They both shuddered in relief.

She was wet, relaxed and ready for him. He was thankful this part of their relationship at least was easy when everything else was so hard.

One day at a time, he reminded himself, and put himself back into this night, into this moment, when her body clasped his tightly and her breath was warm in his ear. He worked her with long, slow strokes and short, deep thrusts. Her hips lifted. Her knees were around his waist.

He raised his head to see her face. She was watching him, her gaze focused. Intent. Unsatisfied.

Convince me.

He swore and pulled out.

Nell frowned, bewildered. "What are you…"

He kissed her throat. He kissed her breast, and then started to lick and suck his way down her squirming torso.

"Oh, no. Really. You don't have to—"

"Shut up," he said, and put his mouth on her.

She moaned.

She tasted wonderful, hot and exotic. He held her down, using his tongue and his teeth, until he felt her shudder and give. Until he felt her gasp and yield. Until her hands clutched his hair and dragged him up to her.

He covered her, pushing inside her as she rocked and twisted under him. Her muscles tightened around him and he almost lost it. But he drove himself, drove them both, taking her harder, deeper, faster.

Her eyes widened. Her breath caught.

"That's it," he murmured. "Come on. Come with me now."

He trapped her hands and held them, held her, as she arched under him and shook apart.

Grateful, spent, he closed his eyes and tumbled with her over the edge of control.

Joe kissed Nell's forehead. "Are you okay?"

Nell quivered. Was she?

She was the one who took care of everyone else. Who took charge at the clinic. Who took responsibility for herself. She held herself accountable for her own sex life, good, bad, indifferent or nonexistent. If you never made demands, you were never disappointed.

But Joe had ignored all that.

He had taken care of her. He'd taken control. And instead of the sky falling, the earth had moved. Her body quaked with the hard, sweet aftershocks of really excellent sex. Joe's determined seduction had assaulted her senses and undermined her defenses. His concern now laid siege to her heart. She didn't know whether to fight or surrender.

Nell looked up into the hard, sharp face of her lover. He was still on top of her, still inside her, their bodies slick and close.

She reached for humor to distance and defend herself. "Ask me the name of the current president," she said.

"Oh, God." Joe raised his weight on his elbows. "Your head. Did I hurt your head?"

Her head was spinning, but not from concussion.

"I can't tell," she said. "Is it still attached to my shoulders?"

The panic faded from Joe's eyes as he smiled. "It appears to be."

"Then I'd say I'm fine."

"Sure? Can I get you anything?" He stroked the hair back from her forehead. The tenderness of his gesture clogged her throat. "A glass of water?"

His offer made her uncomfortable. She was the nurturing one. Wasn't she? All through her childhood, she'd tried hard not to be any trouble. All through her marriage, she'd struggled to be the wife Richard needed. The wife who could keep him straight. The wife who could keep him faithful.

The woman who could earn his love.

She swallowed the lump in her throat. ''I'll get it.''

Joe shook his head. ''You don't have to.''

He kissed her and rolled away.

And there it was. With Joe, she didn't have to do anything. Didn't have to be anything. She could be tired or hurt or cranky or unresponsive and he would cope.

His usurpation of her usual role made her feel cherished. Vulnerable.

Inadequate.

He wanted to take care of her, but he wouldn't accept the same. He didn't need her.

And she needed…

Nell watched Joe pad naked into the bathroom, his features edged with yellow light. Even his limp didn't disguise his natural male grace, his lean hips and broad shoulders, his smooth back and hairy thighs.

Her eyes swam with sudden, unexpected tears. Her chest tightened with sudden, unexpected fear.

Maybe she could live with losing her control.

But how would she survive losing her heart?

Chapter 15

"What do you want to do for dinner tonight?" Joe asked as he dropped Nell off in front of the clinic two days later.

It was such a couples' question. *Hi, honey, I'm home. What's for dinner?*

Nell shivered with pleasure and misgiving. Did she really want to establish a domestic routine with Joe after only two days? She had been married before. She wasn't eager to repeat her mistakes.

On the other hand, Joe wasn't anything like Richard. She could trust him. She did.

One day at a time, she reminded herself, and leaned from her seat to kiss him. "Why don't you pick me up around seven? We'll figure it out from there."

He reached across her to open her door from the inside. He smelled like aftershave and, faintly, of tobacco. "It's Friday. I thought the clinic was only open late Mondays and Thursdays."

"It is. But I'm still catching up on paperwork from when I was out."

"How about catching up on some sleep?"

She arched her eyebrows. "Oh, are we going to sleep tonight?"

"Funny, Dolan. Now get out of here before I get a ticket for blocking traffic."

"I know a guy whose brother's on the force. He could probably get you off."

"Out," Joe ordered.

Nell's smile lasted until she reached the reception desk and discovered Billie tight-lipped and furious because Jim Fletcher had blown off her nine-year-old nephew's appointment.

"Did he tell you why?" Nell asked Melody, who had apparently delivered the news.

The office manager flushed a dull, unbecoming red. "He said he wasn't feeling well this morning."

Oh, no, honey, Nell thought. Was she covering up for the handsome doctor? Or sleeping with him?

"All right. Call his patients and see who can be rescheduled. Give his urgent-care appointments to me or Dr. Nguyen. Billie, how is Trevor?"

"Hurting," Billie said flatly.

"Another pain episode?"

"Same one."

Nell winced in sympathy. "I'm sorry. Do you want me to see him?"

"What good will that do?" Billie snapped, and went to draw a PKU test on a newborn.

Nell stared after her, stricken.

"I put a copy of yesterday's deposit slip on your desk," Melody said, covering the awkward moment.

"Joe couriered over a big donation somebody dropped off at the paper. You should see."

"I'll look at it over lunch," Nell promised.

But she spent her lunchtime writing up notes on her doubled patient load instead. Stanley Vacek was back after lunch, glaring at her from beneath his bushy eyebrows and complaining his new pills made him tired all the time.

Nell listened, nodded and checked his cholesterol and blood sugar levels.

"I read in the paper you don't have any money," Vacek said accusingly.

Since Joe's article appeared, a number of patients had expressed concern about the clinic's future.

Nell smiled reassuringly. "We're going to be around a long time, Mr. Vacek. And donations are actually up in the past couple of days. Don't you worry about us. Are you experiencing any difficulty breathing?"

"No."

"Let's have a listen, anyway," she suggested.

The flood of patients and paperwork continued unabated through the afternoon. At four o'clock, Nell was trying to explain to a victim of the latest flu strain why antibiotics would not make her feel better when Melody stuck her head in the door.

"Can I talk to you a second?"

Nell stepped into the hall. "Can it wait? Because—"

"Detective Ward is here to see you," said Melody in a rush. "I put him in your office."

Her anxiety was contagious. "I'll be there as soon as I've finished with Mrs. Chatterjee."

But when Nell turned the corner to her office a few

minutes later, Kevin Ward was standing with his hands clasped behind his back, scanning the papers scattered on her desk.

Nell bit back anger. "Can I help you, Detective?"

The neat-haired Ward pivoted and looked her up and down. "Are you planning to confess?"

Nell's heart beat faster. "Since I haven't done anything illegal, I can't see how a confession could help you."

"That was a joke, Ms. Dolan."

Neither of them laughed.

"I have a few follow-up questions for you," Ward said, thumbing through his notebook. His gaze sharpened on her face. "If you don't mind."

A weight descended on Nell's chest, making it difficult to breathe. What could she say? She didn't have anything to hide. Except her suspicions.

"I don't have much time."

"Would you prefer to do this at the station? At your convenience, of course."

It was a threat, pleasantly and professionally delivered.

Nell shook her head. "I suppose I could take a few minutes."

Ward smiled. "I appreciate it. What can you tell me about the ten thousand four hundred and thirty-five dollars deposited to your account yesterday afternoon?"

Her mouth dried. "What?"

"Ten thousand four hundred and thirty-five dollars," Ward repeated. "Ten thousand in cash. Deposited to your account yesterday afternoon."

Her mind raced. What had Melody said? *I put a copy of yesterday's deposit slip on your desk.*

Nell looked down at the clutter on her desk and up at Ward. "How would you know about donations made to my account, Detective?"

He smiled. "Plain-view doctrine, Ms. Dolan. But what really caught my eye was today's editorial thanking all the generous people of Chicago who sent donations in care of the paper. Large cash donations. A real windfall for you, isn't it? That kind of money."

Joe's words came back to her. *Drug deals are cash transactions. Ward's going to look for any discrepancies in your cash flow. Unusual windfalls? Big purchases? Expensive habits?*

Nell moistened her lips. "Of course we're happy with the publicity and the donations. But ten thousand dollars isn't all that much."

Ward raised his eyebrows. "I must be in the wrong line of work. It seems like a lot to me. What would you call a lot of money?"

"I only meant... It is a lot of money, but we do receive corporate donations and charitable grants in the thousands and tens of thousands. It's not that unusual."

"And is it usual for those donations to be made anonymously through a third party? Large cash donations just stuffed in an envelope? Without getting a receipt for a tax deduction?"

She was doing this all wrong, Nell realized, watching Ward's smug, impassive face. She shouldn't be trying to defend herself with logic. She should be indignant, horrified, shocked. She should demand an explanation. Insist on a lawyer. That was what innocent people did.

But Nell had been through this before. She wasn't shocked. Only deeply afraid.

Ward planted a hip on a corner of her desk as if he owned it. "Where do you think all that cash came from, Miss Dolan? Can I call you Eleanor?"

"Nell," she said distractedly. This was awful. He didn't just suspect her of drug fraud. He thought she was laundering money. "I suppose the newspaper article…"

"Inspired a fit of charity?"

"Something like that."

"Or guilt?"

She raised her chin. "I wouldn't know. Is there a purpose to these questions, Detective?"

"I just wanted to give you the chance to tell me your side of the story," Ward said. "Any insights, any theories…?"

He waited long moments while her heart beat drummed in her ears.

"No?" He stood. "Then I guess that's everything for now. You might not want to plan any trips for a little while."

He headed for the door.

Nell forced herself to breathe.

"Oh, one other thing," Ward said, turning around at the last moment like Columbo. "I reached out to the state licensing board today. You'll be getting a call from them in the morning, but I wanted you to hear this from me. Your DEA authorization is revoked. Pending the results of this investigation, they're suspending your ability to prescribe."

Not a bad day, Joe thought, rolling a cigarette between his thumb and two fingers. Donations kept coming to the *Examiner* building for Nell's clinic. He had a lead on a social-services scam that might pan out for a story. And his editor had called him in this afternoon to tell him they were running the last installment of his series on the front page of the Sunday paper.

No, not a bad day at all.

Joe grinned and stuck the cigarette back in his pocket. He couldn't wait to tell Nell and see her reaction. Hell, he couldn't wait to see her, period. It was getting to be like a habit with him. Put in a day at the office, pick up Nell and go home.

Okay, the office bit still left him cold, but the Nell-and-home part worked fine.

He stopped on the corner by the pawnshop, waiting for a break in the traffic. Maybe he could talk her into packing a bag and spending the weekend at his house. He wanted her to sleep in his bed, to wake in his room, surrounded by things he'd picked up and kept because he liked them. He wanted her to come to Sunday dinner, to laugh in the kitchen with his mother and spar across the table with his brothers. He wanted more linking them than his razor in her medicine cabinet or her toothbrush in a cup by his sink.

The light changed. He stepped from the curb into the street.

She ought to move in with him. That was the most practical solution. He had the bigger house. She had the knack to make it home. He needed her to make it home.

But did she need him?

The lights above the clinic entrance were on, but the front windows were dark. Joe rapped on the glass.

Nell came from the back, a pale shadow in a white

lab coat, and unlocked the dead bolt. She opened the door, and he felt his day twist and right itself with her as its center.

"How do you feel about Indian?" he asked. "There's a place on Devon does great chicken vindaloo."

Nell held on to the door as if she'd fall down if she let go. "I can't tonight. I'm sorry. I should have called."

The back of Joe's neck prickled. "What's the matter?"

Nell's eyes were as wide and blank as a doll's. "I have things I have to do." Her voice trembled.

"Fine," Joe said easily. He stuck his foot over the threshold. "I'll wait."

"I have to clean out my desk."

It sounded like one of those ridiculous excuses a woman used when she didn't want to see you anymore. "I have to wash my hair." "Walk my dog." "Clean out my sock drawer."

Only Nell wasn't joking and Joe wasn't laughing.

"It's the weekend, babe. Can't it wait till you get back on Monday?"

"I'm not coming back."

He took his hands out of his pockets. "What are you talking about?"

She drew a painful breath. "The donations… Detective Ward thinks I'm using donations to the clinic as a way of hiding money I made dealing drugs."

Son of a bitch. "Did he charge you with anything?"

"He notified DPR."

Not good. She was still on probation, implicated in her user husband's drug fraud.

Joe came inside and shut the door firmly behind him. "Did they yank your license?"

She flinched. "They revoked my DEA authorization."

He was badgering her with rapid-fire interview techniques, using his reporter's logic and need to know to hold panic at bay. He knew it, knew it wasn't what she needed, and yet he couldn't seem to stop.

"What does that mean?"

Nell swallowed. "It means I can't prescribe medicine for my patients anymore. I can't do my job."

"Wait. You have nurses working for you who can't prescribe medications, right?"

"Two salaried nurses who are part of medical teams with volunteer doctors," Nell said precisely. "But there has to be one full-time member of the staff who can work autonomously."

He got that. But…

"You could hire a doctor. Or another nurse practitioner. Just until you're cleared."

Her eyes were bleak. "And how long will that take? How much damage will the scandal do in the meantime?"

"What scandal? Who has to know? I'm not going to write about it."

"Even if it's news?"

Her question stopped him like a cane cracked across his shins. If the story broke, if his editor asked him to follow it, would he?

Nell looked away. "Anyway, you're not the only paper in town."

"You're making this bigger than it has to be," Joe argued desperately.

"The board of directors is making it bigger." He

shot her a disbelieving look. "Ward called them," she explained.

Interfering bastard.

"Why?"

"The suggestion was made it would be best for the clinic if I resign."

"Screw that," said Joe. "They can't touch you. They can't fire you without probable cause, and if they do, they've got the kind of scandal they're trying to avoid."

"But I've lost their support. My ability to do my job is compromised. And I'm still under investigation for drug diversion and prescription fraud."

"You'll fight that," Joe said. "You'll beat that."

"I am tired of fighting," Nell said.

It was like hearing Joan of Arc say she didn't feel like storming any castles today. It was like learning there wasn't any Tooth Fairy or Santa Claus. Her abdication frightened Joe more than the case against her.

"Sure, you're tired," Joe said. "That doesn't mean you resign."

"For the good of the clinic," Nell said.

"*You* are good for the clinic. You *are* the clinic. You're its force. You're its heart. Everyone who works here knows it."

"Someone who works here is stealing drugs and trying to pin the blame on me."

And that betrayal, Joe guessed, cut as deeply as anything else. No wonder she felt beat. Anger licked through him at the person who could do this to her.

"You have to trust to the police to figure that out. My brother, Dietz, even Ward. Let the pros do their job."

"This from a man who won't trust his own doctors?"

Joe set his jaw. Even down, even defeated, Nell was dangerous at close quarters. "I'm just saying you can't let what happened in the past keep you from making a difference here. You can't let fear stop you from doing the work you love. Work that makes a difference to this neighborhood. To this city."

Nell's face was white. Her eyes narrowed. "You're letting your fears keep you from making a difference in the world by doing the work you love. Why do I have to be wiser or stronger, more hopeful or more determined than you are?"

"Because..." At a loss for words to tell her what her staunch idealism, her passion and compassion meant to him, he opened his arms wide. "You just are."

"No. I'm not."

"I never thought you were a quitter," he goaded her.

Her head snapped back. "And I never thought you were a hypocrite. But I don't have to listen to you."

Her accusation hit him like mortar fire, stinging, numbing, debilitating.

"You got that right," Joe said, and walked out.

Nell watched him stride away down the street, one shoulder slightly higher than the other because of his limp, and something broke inside her. Her eyes burned. She blinked.

It was too much, their fight on top of everything else, and it was her fault, she was partly responsible, saying those horrible things to him when he was only telling her what she knew. She had to fight. Only she was so tired of fighting.

She was pretty sick of taking responsibility, too.

Joe never looked back.

Her tears fell. She turned out the lights and shuffled back to her office, misery dragging her steps and burning in her chest. Her credibility with the state licensing board was down the tubes. Her career was in the toilet. Everything she had struggled to build or accomplish in the past two years was about to be flushed away, and no one believed or supported her.

Joe had, a tiny voice reminded her.

She pushed the thought away, hugging her grievance and self-pity tight.

No, he hadn't. She had needed his comfort and understanding, and he had battered her with questions. Plied her with solutions. Pushed her to think and act when she wanted to scream and cry. She couldn't be what he wanted.

Nell sank into her chair and covered her face with her hands. She wasn't strong enough. She wasn't good enough.

She closed her eyes. Tears seeped under her lashes.

She was still sitting, sandbagged, when she heard a noise from the front. A click. A scrape. For one second, she thought *Joe,* and wild hope expanded her chest.

But of course it wasn't Joe. She'd pushed Joe away. Whoever it was was already inside, and Joe didn't have a key.

Alone in her office, Nell wiped hastily at her eyes. She had locked the door, hadn't she?

It could be Melody. The office manager had a key.

Or the cleaning service. The timing was right.

But some instinct, some caution kept Nell from calling out. She pushed to her feet. Were those voices? Her heartbeat quickened.

Instead of taking the hall to the waiting room, she went the other way, past the nurses' station, through the office area, to the patient registration desk.

It was dark, but she could still see Billie. Billie had a key. There were two men with her. Strangers. Patients?

But Nell knew they were not. Her stomach rose to her throat. She looked down for the panic button.

They saw her behind the counter and stopped.

One of the men, a dark bandana tied over his hair, turned his head toward Billie and growled, ''You said nobody would be here.''

Chapter 16

He'd tried to help her, and she'd called him a hypocrite.

Joe hunched his shoulders, shoving his hands deep in his jacket pockets. Damn it, he was no good at this. He should never have gotten involved. If he hadn't featured Nell in that article, she wouldn't have been hit with those donations. Ward wouldn't suspect her of hiding drug money, and the licensing board would have left her alone.

His feet pounded the pavement, jarring his bones, punishing his ankle. He'd screwed up. No wonder she was angry.

He didn't blame her for feeling tired and discouraged. He could forgive her for speaking out of frustration and fear. What he couldn't forgive—or forget, either, Christ, he would never forget the look on her face—was her being right. Right about him.

His abused ankle let him down as he stepped off the curb. He stumbled.

You're letting your fears keep you from making a difference in the world. Keep you from doing the work you love.

Joe raised his head. He was almost at Flynn's. The beer signs in the window glowed like a promise in the dark.

Damn right he was afraid. Not of the surgery itself but of its aftermath.

He was afraid of losing himself again in a fog of pills and booze.

He was afraid of losing Nell. Of disappointing her.

But most of all, he was afraid of failing her.

She wouldn't listen to him. She wouldn't let him help.

Joe stopped on the sidewalk in front of the bar. Which left him, really, with only one option.

Nell hated being afraid. Hated being vulnerable. She really hated being out of control.

She took a deep breath and shifted toward the panic button under the counter, trying not to provoke a reaction. "Billie? What's going on?"

But the other nurse wouldn't meet her eyes.

Misgiving shivered up Nell's spine.

Don't overreact, she told herself. This was Billie, after all, who loved her nephew and fought for every one of her patients. Billie, who teased Nell about her lack of a love life and came running when she cracked her head on the floor. Billie, who this afternoon had trashed the licensing board's decision to revoke Nell's DEA authorization. Billie wouldn't hurt her.

On the other hand, the two guys with her looked as if they might.

Nell eased another step closer to the counter, her fatigue fading as adrenaline kicked in. Her brain started processing details, descriptions. One of the men was big and one was little. Well, skinny. The big one had a bandana tied around his head. The skinny one had three dots tattooed at the corner of his eye and a sneer.

"Who's the bitch?" he asked.

"It doesn't matter," Billie said. "She isn't staying."

A fist squeezed Nell's heart. Any hope she had that her friend was an unwilling accomplice snuffed out.

"Yeah, she is." He raised his arm. Oh God, he was holding a gun, a stubby black handgun, no compensation issues for this guy.... Casually, he pointed it at her, which had the unpleasant effect of making it look much larger. "Don't move."

She froze, still a yard away from the panic button, her palms sweating with fear, her heart pounding with betrayal.

"She Dolan?"

Billie didn't answer.

"I *asked* you." Skinny's voice cracked like a gunshot. "Is she Dolan?"

Nell swallowed her heart, which had lodged in her throat. "What does it matter? What do you want?"

"If you're Dolan, you can write more prescriptions. Real ones."

"She can't," Billie said. "I told you that won't work anymore."

He rounded on her, his movements jerky. "You told me a lot of things. Like how nobody would be here. You about as dumb and useless as your crack-whore sister.''

Nell's mind worked frantically, trying to make sense of an unthinkable situation. Billie's sister? Trevor's mother. This must be the lameass boyfriend, the one Billie always spoke of with such scorn. Why would she help him? For her sister's sake? For Trevor's?

Nell edged closer to the counter, feeling with her foot for the button on the floor.

Skinny pinned her with a look. ''You got keys?''

Nell's mouth went dry. He wanted the keys to the pharmacy.

''You don't need her keys,'' Billie said sharply, drawing his attention. ''You're going to make it look like a break-in, you said. You don't need her.''

He smiled, a wide, flat smile that didn't reach his eyes. ''Wrong. Now that I've got her, I don't need you.''

Nell watched in disbelief as he straightened his arm. The arm with the gun.

Billie set her hands on her hips. ''You have got to be kidding.''

He shot her. The bullet took her high in the chest, and her body crashed back into a row of patient chairs.

Nell gasped. Dropping under the counter's protective overhang, she smacked her palm as hard as she could on the panic button. She was shaking. *Billie, my God, Billie...*

''Get her,'' ordered Skinny.

Crawling on her hands and knees, Nell scrambled to the nurses' station. Her office. If she could make it to her office, she had a chance. The door locked.

They'd have to shoot it open. But, oh, Billie was lying bleeding on the waiting-room floor…

Big Guy launched himself at the patient registration desk, straight across the counter. Nell lurched to her feet. She ran three steps before he grabbed a handful of her hair. Yanked. Her neck jerked back. Her head exploded. Releasing his grip on her hair, he threw her into the wall. She bounced off cinder block and rolled into the doorway of Exam One.

White hot pain, shot through with colors, blinded her. She couldn't get up, couldn't think, couldn't breathe…

Billie. Billie couldn't breathe either.

Nell started to crawl again.

A boot came down hard on her back, squashing her to the floor like a cockroach. She grunted as the breath whooshed out of her lungs.

"Where's the keys?" a voice demanded.

She couldn't tell whose. Didn't care. Her brain was groggy. Her jaw was out of whack. Her cheek mashed against the cold linoleum. She couldn't have answered if she wanted to.

The boot lifted. A hand tangled in the coat bunched over her back—not her hair, she was grateful not to be hauled up by her hair—and spun her around. The overhead light jumped on. Nell closed her eyes in pain and protest.

He shoved his face into hers. The little black dots swung up and down, gang symbols for *mi vida loca,* my crazy life.

He asked again, "Where are the damn keys?"

Nell licked her lips. "I don't know."

Bam. He backhanded her into the padded examination table. She clung to it so she wouldn't slide to the floor, tasting blood in her mouth from a cut inside her cheek.

How long before the police responded to the panic alarm? How long until Billie bled out and died? Nell could hear her friend's breathing, grunting shallow rasps as her chest filled with blood.

Unless that was her own breathing. It was hard to tell.

"Get me the keys," Skinny said, his voice low with menace.

He could have them. She could feel their jagged edges in her lab-coat pocket, poking into her stomach as she sprawled across the table.

Who did she think she was protecting, anyway? The clinic? The public? Her friendly neighborhood drug addicts? Why should she give a damn about them, when her head felt split in two and her jaw throbbed and her ribs ached and Billie, her friend who had betrayed her, lay bleeding on the waiting-room floor?

Nell wedged a hand under her lab coat. Her fingers closed over the keys.

I never thought you were a quitter.

"Get them yourself," she spat, and raised herself on her elbows and dropped the keys into the biohazard bag on the wall.

Skinny's eyes were flat and cold. "You're gonna be real sorry you did that," he promised.

She bet.

She opened her mouth to scream.

"Hey, baby." She knew *that* voice, that deep, smoke-roughened voice with its under note of humor, now strangely slurred. "Where's the party?"

A great surge of relief and terror swept over her.

"Joe!" she yelled. "Get the hell out of here!"

Skinny swore and dragged her to the door to see outside.

She sobbed once. Oh God. Oh, no. Not Joe.

He was framed by the opening above the registration desk, standing just inside the entrance, grinning at her sheepishly.

"Now, honey, don't be mad," he said, shuffling forward.

A different fear hollowed Nell's chest. A different prayer spun in her brain. He wasn't... He hadn't...

Joe peered at her, bemused, totally ignoring Billie's body, crumpled in the shadows. "It was only a couple of drinks," he said plaintively.

Nell's face went numb. Her heart went cold.

He *was* and he *had.*

She was devastated. Betrayed. Bereft.

You are nothing at all like my ex-husband, she had said.

And she'd believed it. Believed in him.

Joe smiled at her gently, swaying on his feet.

"Get rid of him," Skinny ordered.

Bandana man lumbered through the door between the pharmacy and patient checkout.

"Whoa, big fella," Joe greeted him cheerfully, but Nell didn't hear any more, because Skinny dragged her back into Exam One.

"Joe, run!" she screamed, but he couldn't run. He was lame and he was drunk. Frantic, she cursed and kicked and cried.

Her captor lifted his gun. Leveled it. Even though her heart was broken, even though her life was over, Nell fought to free herself from his grip on her elbow.

But he wasn't aiming at her. Pointing the gun at the biohazard bag on the wall, he fired.

The report echoed off the walls. Nell shrieked and cowered. The stench of cordite and melted plastic filled the room.

Skinny pointed his gun at the floor, where the keys gleamed in a mess of discarded swabs and used syringes, rusty with blood and black with burn residue.

"Pick them up," he ordered. "Or your boyfriend's next."

Joe.

Defeated, Nell dropped to her knees. Trembling with fear and fury, she raked through the filthy gauze and blasted plastic. Her heart shook with pity and a terrible loss.

He was going to shoot Joe anyway. He was going to shoot them both.

Nell expected the second blast. Was braced for it. Even so, she gasped and jumped at the sound of the shot, so loud, so close.

Loud enough it almost covered the shout, "Halt. Police."

She twisted as Skinny toppled forward, eyes wide, a neat round hole in his back.

She looked up, over his fallen body. In the doorway, Mike Reilly lowered his gun. His face was white and sheened with sweat. His expression was grim.

Nell realized he hadn't given her attacker any time to respond, any chance to surrender. She watched the blood pool under the body on her examining-room floor and was glad.

And then instinct and training kicked in, and she scrambled forward on her knees, checking his neck for a pulse. It was there, thready, beating. He was alive. She grabbed latex gloves and a stack of absorbent pads from a supply drawer.

"Nell? Are you okay?" Mike asked.

"Fine," Nell snapped over her shoulder. She grappled with the gloves, tugged and rolled her scrawny assailant onto his side. He groaned, his eyes rolling up. He had a gaping hole in his shoulder, and she thought his scapula was broken.

"Find Joe," she said urgently. "And Billie. There's a man in the waiting room and he's got Joe."

"No, he doesn't." Mike holstered his weapon. Nell wadded padding into the exit wound and applied pressure, struggling to staunch the flow of blood. "Tom came in the front while I went around back. Joe was supposed to wait for our backup, but the damn fool wouldn't stay put. We were almost in position when we heard the shot."

Nell raised her head, distracted from her fight to save the life of the man who had tried to kill her. "How is he?"

"Joe? He's down. But—"

Down? Her heart squeezed. She threw another pair of gloves at Mike, hitting him at the waist. She wasn't exposing Joe's little brother to HIV. "Get these on and get pressure on this shoulder. I have to check on Joe and Billie."

Adrenaline surged, lifting her like a great swell over pain and past panic. She didn't think. She reacted the way she had been trained to do. Loading her arms with more pads, more gloves—was it too late? was she too late?—she stumbled toward the front room. As she pushed through the door, she heard the rising wail of sirens.

Joe slumped against one wall, legs straight out in

front of him. Sitting. Conscious? Alive, anyway. The big thug was down and handcuffed on the floor. Beneath a broken line of chairs, Tom Dietz bent over Billie.

Just for a second, Nell wavered.

But she knew the principles of triage. The more serious injury got treated first. Always. She ran toward the line of chairs.

Billie was bad. A glance confirmed she needed fluids, oxygen, blankets, surgery and more help than Nell could provide. But before Nell could stagger to the acute-care room to grab an IV bag and a line, the door burst open and the blessed paramedics charged in and swarmed over the room. Two teams.

Nell sagged back out of their way as they jumped to their jobs, sending up a silent prayer of thanks to God and Tom Dietz's police radio.

Her legs shook. She was shaking all over, with shock and reaction. She needed to sit down. But not yet. Not yet. Peeling off her bloody gloves, she lurched across the room, clutching at seat backs for support, to where Joe slouched against the wall. A paramedic squatted beside him.

Joe's head tipped back. His eyes were closed. He looked like hell, his face the color of melted wax, his strong features slack with pain, and she loved him so much and resented him so much her heart was breaking in two.

Richard used to swear each time was the last time. If only she would take him back, he'd stay clean. If only she would trust him, he would never use again. Joe had been different. He'd never promised her anything. But she had believed in him to the bottom of

her soul, and the betrayal of her hopes hurt more than
the crack on her head.

As Nell reached them, the medic pushed up Joe's
sleeve and pulled out a syringe.

"What are you giving him?" she asked more
sharply than she intended.

Joe's eyes opened. She couldn't bring herself to
look at him. She didn't want to see that sharp blue
gaze clouded with alcohol, didn't want him to read
he disappointment in her own eyes.

"Just something for the pain," the medic said.
"Hey, is any of that blood you're wearing yours?"

Nell shook her head. "Give him Toradol. And
check his blood alcohol level."

"Nell, it's okay," Joe said quietly.

She patted his arm, needing the reassurance of his
warm, living body. But she still couldn't meet his
eyes.

"Toradol is a nonnarcotic analgesic. And you have
to be careful of drug interactions with alcohol."

"Fine. Toradol is fine," he said gently. "But I
haven't been drinking. You don't have to worry about
my alcohol level or anything else. *Is* any of that blood
yours?"

"No." She didn't know. "I don't think so."

She couldn't think. She hardly dared to hope. If he
wasn't drunk, then what was wrong with him? "Joe,
when you came in…"

"I figured a stumbling drunk was less of a threat."
His lids drifted shut. "I was right about the stumbling
part."

"But… What happened to you?"

His mouth curved. "First they tore my legs off, and

they threw them over there! Then they tore my chest out, and they threw—''

"No alcohol in his system," the medic said. "Is he delusional?"

Understanding bloomed in her chest, crowding the air from her lungs. "No, he thinks he's the Scarecrow in *The Wizard of Oz*," Nell snapped. "Joe!"

He opened his eyes. His blue gaze focused on her, bright with pain and fever. "No brain," he said. "But my heart is all yours."

She sobbed with guilt and relief and fear and a terrible joy. "Oh, Joe."

He reached out and took her hand, lacing his fingers with hers. She fell back on her butt and cried like a baby, hugging their clasped hands to her chest.

Mike came up behind her and stood over them. "What the hell happened to you?" he demanded. "You were supposed to wait outside."

"He decided to provide a diversion," Tom Dietz reported. "Waltzed in while I radioed for backup and then took on the big guy when I came through the door. Gave me a chance to get in, and we got the cuffs on the guy eventually. But your brother got beat up some."

Mike nodded. "Always did have a glass jaw."

"This ankle's broken," the medic said. "It will have to be reset."

"Don't you touch him," Nell said fiercely.

The two cops and the paramedic looked at her in surprise.

Joe laughed and held more tightly to her hand. "It's okay, Dolan. I'm okay."

And from the lightness in his voice and the light in his eyes, she saw he finally believed it.

Chapter 17

"No coffee," Nell said firmly, confiscating the large take-out cup from Will at the door. "Nothing to eat or drink for at least eight hours prior to surgery."

Watching her from his hospital bed, Joe thought she looked tired. The fluorescent lights overhead bleached her face of color. The bruises stood out vividly on her jaw. She should be home in her own bed, not waiting attendance on him and running interference with his family. But even battered, bruised and exhausted, Nell was determined. And still so beautiful she made his heart ache.

Will tried to hold on to the cup. "It's not for Joe. It's for me."

"Give it up," Mike advised. "The woman's ruthless. She took my doughnuts. And after I saved her life, too."

Joe wouldn't blame Nell if she bailed on him. On all of them. She didn't need this crap.

"You did save my life," she said. "I'm grateful."

Mike turned dull red. "I didn't mean...Tom was the one who caught the call. And Joe may be a moron, but he did create a diversion. I just..."

"Shot the guy," Will supplied helpfully.

Joe knew Mike hadn't had a choice. He also knew, whether Mike admitted it or not, that the shooting would have consequences.

"How's he doing? The guy?"

"Delbert Jackson. He's recovering." Mike shrugged. "He gets transferred to the prison hospital today."

"And Billie Parker?"

"Can't be moved yet," Nell said. "She's still in ICU."

Joe raised his eyebrows. "And you know this because...?"

Nell stuck out her chin. "I visited her yesterday."

Yeah, she would. Nell would never abandon one of her lame ducks. The thought was vaguely disquieting. Especially since she had just taken on his entire family. He wished they'd clear the hell out of here so he could tell her... So he could ask her...

He couldn't ask her anything. Not now. Not when it was possible she'd say "yes" for all the wrong reasons.

"Didn't she try to frame you for drug fraud or something?" Will asked.

"Not really," said Nell. "Her nephew, Trevor, has sickle-cell disease, which requires an aggressive pain-treatment plan. Billie kept insisting Trevor had developed a tolerance to pain medication, but Dr.

Fletcher felt he'd already prescribed the maximum dosage. What none of us knew, including Trevor's mother, was that her boyfriend—''

''Jackson,'' Mike interrupted.

''The guy you shot,'' Will said.

''Yeah.''

''Anyway, the boyfriend was stealing Trevor's medication all along,'' Nell continued. ''So Trevor was in a lot of pain. Billie started taking drugs for him from the clinic pharmacy.''

''Until you discovered the discrepancy in the pharmacy's records and called in the police,'' said Joe.

Nell nodded.

''So then she stopped stealing?'' Will asked.

''She wanted to,'' Nell said, still defending her friend.

She never gave up on the people she cared about. Even when she thought he'd tumbled off the wagon, she hadn't let the paramedic shoot him full of dope. But was she loyal out of love or duty or some wierd personality tic? And did he even want to know?

Mike snorted. ''Her story is that the boyfriend found out and threatened to turn her in unless she kept him supplied with drugs. He leaned on her to steal Nell's prescription pad—''

''Under protest,'' Nell said.

''Whatever. She took the pad and provided Jackson with a list of patients who were prescribed pain meds. We can't prove she actually forged the prescriptions, but it's a cinch she knew Nell's signature.''

''Trevor was still in pain,'' Nell said. ''And Billie was scared about what would happen to him or his mother if she lost her job.''

''Who made the pickups?'' Joe asked.

"Jackson and his buddies. It was a sweet system," Mike said.

"So, if it was such a sweet system, how come he broke into the clinic?" asked Will.

"I told Billie I was resigning and that my DEA authorization was being revoked," Nell admitted.

"Which meant Jackson was about to lose his source," Mike said. "He figured he'd get in that night, wipe out the pharmacy, and hope the thefts were blamed on Nell. Only she screwed up his plans by sticking around."

"Why did you stick around?" Will asked.

"I had to clean out my desk."

"And Joe was helping," Will said dryly.

Joe set his jaw. No, he had chosen that low moment in his lover's life to accuse her of not trying hard enough to fight.

"Actually, Joe left," Nell said. "He came back."

"Why?" asked Mike.

Joe stiffened. He was so not going there. Not with his brothers listening in, and his parents due any moment. "What?"

"I didn't think about it at the time, but why did you go back?"

Nell turned her head to look at him.

He felt the weight of expectation in her eyes and started to sweat. This was not the way he wanted to tell her. It was not the way she deserved to hear.

He couldn't dump the burden of his feelings on her now, when she was tied to his side by pity and professional obligation.

"It doesn't matter now," he said.

Will grinned. "That means it's good."

"Yeah?" Mike looked interested. "How good?"

Will caught him casually around the neck and dragged him two steps toward the door. ''Good enough that he doesn't want an audience, peanut.''

''Hey.'' Struggling, Mike drove an elbow into his older brother's midsection. ''You're assaulting an officer, goon face.''

''So arrest me,'' Will suggested casually.

''Is this any way to behave in the hospital?'' Mary Reilly stood in the doorway, her tone severe and her eyes worried.

Her sons untangled themselves. Mike tugged on his uniform jacket.

''No, ma'am.''

''Hi, Mom.''

Ted stomped over to the television in the corner and flicked on the morning news.

Joe was on edge. He appreciated the effort his parents had made to be here. He did. But right now they were a distraction to him and an added responsibility for Nell.

She was talking to his mother now, interpreting whatever it was the doctors had told her. All weekend, while Joe had been a useless lump confined to bed, his family had looked to Nell for answers, for explanations, for reassurance.

''It's a precaution,'' she was saying. ''If at any time during the surgery the spinal block doesn't work, the doctors need to be able to put Joe under fast.''

Ted turned his head as a commercial came on. ''Then why not put him under in the first place? Seems like a waste of time to me.''

Joe watched the question sink in with his brothers and take root in his mother's eyes. A terrible anticipation twisted his gut.

''There are always risks associated with general anesthesia,'' Nell said gently, avoiding the real issue. ''Allergies, adverse reactions…''

''He didn't have any adverse reactions before,'' Ted said. ''Why don't his doctors use whatever they used on him then?''

Nell took a deep breath. Preparing to lie for him?

And Joe knew he couldn't let her do it. This was one question she couldn't answer for him. One burden she shouldn't have to carry. One sin she shouldn't need to cover up.

She had been forced to lie and to suffer to protect her ex-husband.

He'd be damned before he'd let her do the same for him. He had to speak up. For her sake. For his.

''They aren't using the same drugs because I asked them not to,'' he said.

Nell turned to him, protective, troubled. ''Joe, I don't think this is the time—''

''It's past time,'' he said grimly. ''The question came up. They deserve the truth. And so do you.''

Mary's face creased in bewilderment. ''What truth? What are you talking about?''

Nell crossed the room to stand beside Joe's bed.

He took her small, strong hand and held on tight. Maybe that made him weak, dependent, but he wasn't sure he could make it through what he needed to say without her support.

''I asked the doctors to find an alternative to general anesthesia because I'm a morphine addict,'' he said, forcing the words from his tight throat. ''I got addicted to painkillers in Iraq, and I made the situation worse by drinking. I can't take any narcotics. Ever. I can't drink, either, ever again.''

He waited for their disbelief, their disappointment and disapproval.

The hospital room was silent and still except for the buzz and flicker of the florescent lights.

"Well, that explains the leftover beer every time we get together," Mike said after a moment.

Will cuffed their younger brother lightly on the back of the head. "It explains a lot more than that, dumbass."

"Language," Mary said, but automatically, as if her mind was someplace else. There were tears in her eyes. "Joey," she said, using her name for him when he was a little boy. "Are you sure?"

"Of course he's sure," Ted snapped, lumbering from his chair. "You think he's going to make something like that up?"

Nell opened her mouth. He squeezed her hand in warning. He didn't need her to stand between him and his father's anger.

Ted stopped at the foot of his son's bed. His broad shoulders were bunched, his big head slightly lowered.

"We've always been proud of you," he said gruffly. "That hasn't changed. You're doing the right thing."

Joe sat, stunned. *The right thing*. It was the highest praise Ted Reilly could give.

"Come on, Mary," Ted said to his wife. "Let's get a cup of coffee."

"But, Joe..." Mary protested.

"We'll see Joe after the surgery," Ted said. "I need a cup of coffee now."

Mary stood obediently, her face still crumpled with distress.

"Ma." Joe stopped her with a touch on her arm. "I'm sorry. I love you."

Her eyes overflowed with tears. But she bent and kissed him on the forehead, the way she used to when she tucked him into bed at night. "I love you, too." Her voice wavered. "We'll... We'll see you soon."

She followed her husband from the room.

Will coughed.

Mike hunched his shoulders. "You can let go of your girlfriend's hand now. Before you, like, break her fingers."

Joe realized he was indeed gripping Nell's hand too tight. Not hard enough to crush bone, but enough to cut off her circulation.

"Sorry," he said, releasing her abruptly.

"You have nothing to be sorry for," Nell said.

That sounded good. But he knew better.

Will cleared his throat.

"Well..."

Mike shifted awkwardly. "We better go before they throw us out."

It wasn't his brothers' way to say what they felt. Joe was the one who worked and played with words. And even he tended to lose them in moments of high emotion.

"Right," he said. "See you."

They clasped hands. Patted shoulders.

"Later, man."

It was a promise. *We'll be here.*

Joe nodded. "Later."

It was a guarantee. *I'll be fine.*

He wished he believed it.

Mike gave him a half salute, and they were gone.

"I like your family," Nell said, moving away from his bed.

He stared at her back, frustrated. "They like you."

The hell with timing. She was here. They were alone. He loved her, damn it, and if he couldn't tell her now he was as big a coward as she'd accused him of being.

He braced himself. "Nell…"

"Now that we're alone, we should talk about what you can expect in the OR," she said.

He scowled. "The teaching nurse already went over all that."

"Did she explain that in addition to the spinal block, the doctor will inject the surgical site with a long-lasting local anesthetic?"

"Yeah." He tried again. "Nell…"

"Are you worried about pain? Because there will be Toradol in your IV, and you can receive injections every six to eight hours, as well."

And that's when Joe got it. Family compliments aside, Nell was fighting to keep this conversation from getting too personal.

Misgiving ripped him. Maybe she wanted to keep his focus this morning on him. That would fit her nurturing nature.

Maybe his upcoming procedure had finally made her stop seeing him as a man and start thinking of him as a patient. He hated that, but he could understand it.

A hole opened in his chest. Or maybe dealing with his family, his surgery and his recovery had forced Nell to face the truth.

Maybe she didn't want him enough. Maybe she didn't care about him enough. God knew she didn't need him. She'd already wasted too many years on her jerk of an ex-husband. Maybe she'd wised up enough to know she didn't want to tie herself to an alcoholic cripple for the rest of her life.

But would she tell him so before he went under the knife? Joe's gut clenched. Hell, no. Not Nell, with her big heart and high ideals and her own personal collection of lame ducks.

She touched the side of his face, her fingers smooth against his stubble. Her veins were blue inside her wrist. Her scent was warm and reassuring against the frightening antiseptic smells of the hospital.

"Do you need anything?" she asked. A nurse's question, but her eyes were soft and seeking.

You, he thought. *I need you.*

But he couldn't say it. He wouldn't force her to choose between telling the truth and sparing his feelings.

Even if she cared for him, what if the upcoming operation was a failure? Joe didn't doubt for a minute that Nell would stick by him through sickness, health and disfiguring disability. But he couldn't ask her to do it. Not until he knew if he would ever walk again. Not until she knew what she was getting into. She deserved that much, at least.

And so he gave her the answer he thought she wanted to hear, the answer that wouldn't place another demand on her, another burden of guilt.

"I'm fine," he lied. "Don't worry about me."

Don't worry?

Nell glanced again at the blank-faced clock on the wall, her hands clenched in her lap and her heart lodged in her throat.

She knew Joe had the best orthopedic surgeon in Chicago realigning his ankle. She'd met twice with the anesthesiologist to ensure his wishes were followed to the letter. She'd taken every professional precaution for a successful surgical outcome.

But none of that mattered now that she was relegated to the waiting room with the rest of Joe's family. Nell hadn't felt so scared, so bereft, since her mother had died.

Moistening her lips, she tried to compose a prayer, a dizzy, dry-mouthed bargain with God.

Let him be all right, she prayed, and I won't ask for anything else. Just help him get through this, and I'll settle for anything he has to give me.

Mary Reilly reached over and patted her clasped hands. "He's fine," she said. "Don't you worry."

At the echo of Joe's words, Nell pulled herself together. It was her job to provide reassurance and support. She couldn't possibly let herself be comforted by Joe's mother.

"I'm not worried." She forced a smile. "I'm just so sorry he has to go through this again. That you all have to go through this."

"He needed the surgery anyway," said Will. "Now he's getting it."

Mike rocked back on his heels, his hands in his pockets. "Thanks to you."

Nell winced. "You mean, because he was reinjured coming to my rescue."

"No, because you got the drug thing out in the open and dealt with it," Mike corrected her.

Nell looked anxiously around the circle of faces. "And are you all…okay with that?"

His family was important to Joe. He would need

their support in the coming weeks. But could they come to terms with his addiction?

Mike snorted.

"Do we have a choice?" asked Will.

"Of course we're okay with it," Ted said. "He's our boy."

"He's a good boy." Mary smiled at her husband, her dark eyes shining with tears. "All three are good boys. And Joe…"

"Is going to be okay." A muscle ticked in Mike's jaw. "He's…"

"A tough SOB," Will said.

Mary narrowed her eyes. "Language."

"Let them be," Ted said. "I've heard you say worse."

"Not me," Mary said.

A smile tugged the corner of Mike's mouth. "Dad must be thinking of Will. He always did have a way with words. Smooth bastard."

Will laughed. "Not me. That's Joe."

Listening to their banter, Nell's chest felt so tight she couldn't breathe. And that's when she knew.

She wasn't content to settle anymore. She wanted more. She wanted this. She wanted everything, this unjudging acceptance, this unconditional love.

But of course she couldn't say so.

Joe and his family needed her help. She couldn't make demands now, couldn't burden them with her feelings. Okay, she finally understood she couldn't—shouldn't—have to earn their love, that it had to be given freely. But what if Joe didn't want her, didn't want her love?

She didn't want him to think that her support came with conditions, either.

* * *

Nell shifted her grocery bags to one arm, digging in the pocket of her cloak for the keys to Joe's house. She had bread, salad, an uncooked chicken and a pre-baked apple pie. Everything they needed to celebrate the removal of Joe's plaster bandage and stitches earlier today.

He'd called her at the clinic after his appointment with the physical therapist. He wouldn't walk without crutches for another six weeks, but he'd sounded excited about his progress so far. The surgery had restored the structure of his ankle. Joe was healing.

Which meant that soon, very soon, he wouldn't need her anymore.

Her heart beat up in her throat. She swallowed hard.

This was a good thing, Nell told herself firmly. Tonight could be so much more than a celebration of Joe's medical recovery. It could be the beginning of their new life.

Assuming she had the guts actually to go through with her plan.

She fumbled with the keys. After Joe's discharge from the hospital, she'd moved into his house. For the past two weeks, they'd shared an uneasy domesticity as awkward as it was bittersweet. His family looked in on him during the day. But his nights were hers. Last night, despite his pain and his plaster cast, they'd even managed to make exquisitely careful love, their murmured instructions interspersed by soft gasps and gentle exclamations.

But they didn't talk. They hadn't talked. Nell was afraid to talk.

She was grateful, though, for every moment, every

memory she could hoard away. And maybe the moments would be enough. Enough to sustain her if he
turned her away.

One day at a time, she reminded herself, and
opened the door.

She heard voices. Male voices, boisterous and confident. Joe must have company.

Nell hiked her groceries on her hip and followed
the sound to the living room.

"...be really sorry to lose you," the unfamiliar
voice was saying. "But it's a great opportunity.
Myerson is pumped to have you back."

Nell paused on the threshold. Back? Back where?

"I'm feeling pretty pumped myself," Joe said. He
was sitting on the black leather couch, his leg up and
his expression animated, talking to a man she'd never
met. He looked up and saw her and the welcome on
his face eased the tightness in her chest. "Hi, honey.
Come meet Paul Goodwin, our Metro editor. Paul,
this is Nell."

She couldn't help noticing she didn't have a title
or a label. Not Nell-my-girlfriend or Nell-the-nurse or
Nell-the-love-of-my-life.

"Mr. Goodwin." She shifted her groceries so she
could offer her hand. "It's a pleasure."

So she lied.

Apparently Goodwin didn't notice, because he
shook hands and said, "Paul, please. I didn't mean to
intrude."

"Paul came by to tell me he tracked down your
elusive donor." Joe was smiling, but his eyes were
watchful.

Nell blinked, momentarily distracted. "My...?"

"The guy who stuffed ten grand in an envelope and dropped it off at the paper."

"Oh! Oh, of course. Who…?"

"Patient of yours. Stanley Vacek?"

"Mr. Vacek?" She was dumbfounded. Her grumpy old gnome? "But he doesn't have any money."

Paul Goodwin chuckled. "Don't you believe it. Guy made a fortune on the Russian black market before the fall of communism. Apparently he didn't come forward before this because he didn't want the IRS or INS to know."

Concern pinched Nell. "Is he in trouble?"

"Nope. Nobody's trying to extradite him, and the statute of limitations has expired. He'll have to start paying taxes, though."

Nell's mouth curved. "Well, that's…"

Unbelievable, she thought.

"Wonderful," she said. "Thank you for coming by."

"My pleasure." The editor sounded like he meant it. "It's not every day I get involved with a story that has a happy ending. And of course I wanted to congratulate Joe here on getting his old job back."

Nell's breath stopped. Her heart froze and then shattered like an icicle on the sidewalk.

"His old job?" she repeated faintly.

"Yeah. He's done some great work for us—loved the health insurance series—but I guess our loss is World's gain." He looked at the flowers sticking out of the top of Nell's grocery bag and smiled. "Well, it looks like you two have your own celebration planned. Joe, I'll be seeing you."

"Paul. Thanks for stopping by."

Somehow Nell managed to walk the editor to the

door without screaming or crying or dropping her groceries on the floor.

Joe was sitting up waiting for her return.

"Of course, it will be a while before I can go on assignment," he said as soon as she reappeared. "But Myerson let me know that as soon as I'm mobile he wants me back in the field."

The weight in her arms, the cold whole chicken and bright foolish flowers, dragged on her chest and mocked her hopes.

Breathe, Nell commanded herself. Smile.

Just because Joe was so clearly delighted to get his old job back didn't mean he didn't want her, too. She should be happy for him. She *was* happy for him. He had believed in her when no one else had. He had given her back her faith and her career. She wouldn't grudge him the same. She just needed a moment to absorb the news and adjust her own expectations.

"That's wonderful," she said calmly. "Excuse me while I put these in water."

She escaped into the kitchen, terrified her control would slip. Setting her bags on the counter, she bowed her head, fighting tears.

Joe stood and swung after her on his crutches. "I thought you'd be pleased."

Nell forced herself to move. Briskly, she started unloading groceries onto the counter, trying not to look at him. "I am," she insisted. "I'm just trying to be practical."

He frowned, his sharp blue eyes fixed on her face. "What does that mean?"

Oh, God, she couldn't stand it. Her timing was wrong. Again. It was one thing to decide she wasn't going to settle anymore. It was quite another to confide all her fragile hopes and grand plans to a man who had just announced his eagerness to go half a world away.

It spoiled the mood.

Her hands shook. The lettuce blurred. "I have to fix dinner," she said abruptly. "You need to eat."

"Damn it, Nell." Using his crutches, he pushed himself forward. "Will you stop trying to take care of me and just tell me what's wrong?"

That did it. She broke. She dropped the lettuce and turned to face him, tired of fighting both him and herself.

"I can't," she said. "Don't ask me to. If I stop taking care of you, there's no role for me in your life."

His eyes narrowed. He looked furious. Shaken. "That's bull. I love you."

She hadn't dreamed he would hurl the words at her like stones.

She flinched. "You don't have to say that."

He swore. "Apparently I do.. Obviously I should have said it sooner."

Her heart hammered. "Not if you didn't mean it."

He glared at her. "Of course I mean it. I just didn't want to put you in a position where you'd be forced to say yes or no."

She moistened her dry lips. "Why... Why not?"

"For starters, I didn't know if the surgery was going to be a success. What kind of future could I offer you if I couldn't even walk?"

Her heart pounded. "That doesn't matter to me."

"Well, it does to me," he said through his teeth. "I didn't want to be another obligation you took on."

Did she dare to believe him? Could she bear not to?

"You're not an obligation to me," she whispered.

He shook his head. "You are so damn giving. You deserve so much. More, maybe, than I can give you."

Dread curled her stomach.

"Is this where you give me the let's-be-friends speech?" she asked. "Because I don't think I can take that right now."

"No. Hell, no. I don't want us to be friends, Dolan. But I don't want to be your damn patient, either. I don't want you staying to take care of me."

I don't want you staying. Her heart froze. "How can you think that?" she asked.

"Why wouldn't I think that? That's your job."

Nell had had enough. "It's not my job that's the issue here. What about yours?"

"What about it?"

She spelled it out for him. "You're leaving."

His head came up. His face went still. "Are you asking me to choose between you and going back into the field?" he asked quietly.

"No." She shook her head, frustrated he could know her so well and still not know why she loved him. "I'm glad you have your job back. I'm glad you have your idealism back. You should go make a difference in the world. But when you leave, you're taking my heart with you."

And the separation would probably kill her.

He stared at her. "You don't get it, do you? My heart is here. No matter where I go, no matter what I do, my heart is here with you."

She was weeping as he said, "You are my center. The center of my world. I won't take a permanent posting abroad. I can reduce the length of my assignments. I'll do anything you need to make this work.''

''I don't want you to do anything,'' she said honestly. ''As long as you come home.''

''I will always, always come home to you.''

Balancing on his crutches, he cupped her face. He kissed the tears from her eyes.

''If you'll have me,'' he whispered. ''Will you? Will you marry me, Nell, and live in our house and have our children and be my home and the world to me?''

She drew back her head. Not far. Just enough to look into his eyes. And the answer she found there satisfied her heart.

''That's a pretty articulate proposal, Reilly.''

''Yeah.'' He grinned. ''But it's sincere as hell.''

Deeply content, she said, ''Then I'll have to settle for that.''

''Is that a 'yes'?''

Her smile spilled. ''That is absolutely a 'yes.'''

He kissed her.

And knew, as his arms closed around her, that she would never have to settle for less than she wanted again.

* * * * *

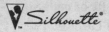

If you enjoyed what you just read,
then we've got an offer you can't resist!

Take 2 bestselling love stories FREE!

Plus get a FREE surprise gift!

Clip this page and mail it to Silhouette Reader Service™

IN U.S.A.	**IN CANADA**
3010 Walden Ave.	P.O. Box 609
P.O. Box 1867	Fort Erie, Ontario
Buffalo, N.Y. 14240-1867	L2A 5X3

YES! Please send me 2 free Silhouette Intimate Moments® novels and my free surprise gift. After receiving them, if I don't wish to receive anymore, I can return the shipping statement marked cancel. If I don't cancel, I will receive 6 brand-new novels every month, before they're available in stores! In the U.S.A., bill me at the bargain price of $3.99 plus 25¢ shipping and handling per book and applicable sales tax, if any*. In Canada, bill me at the bargain price of $4.74 plus 25¢ shipping and handling per book and applicable taxes**. That's the complete price and a savings of at least 10% off the cover prices—what a great deal! I understand that accepting the 2 free books and gift places me under no obligation ever to buy any books. I can always return a shipment and cancel at any time. Even if I never buy another book from Silhouette, the 2 free books and gift are mine to keep forever.

245 SDN DNUV
345 SDN DNUW

Name _____ (PLEASE PRINT) _____

Address _____ Apt.# _____

City _____ State/Prov. _____ Zip/Postal Code _____

* Terms and prices subject to change without notice. Sales tax applicable in N.Y.
** Canadian residents will be charged applicable provincial taxes and GST.
All orders subject to approval. Offer limited to one per household and not valid to current Silhouette Intimate Moments® subscribers.
® are registered trademarks of Harlequin Books S.A., used under license.

INMOM02   ©1998 Harlequin Enterprises Limited

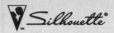

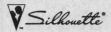

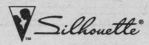 Silhouette®

COMING NEXT MONTH

INTIMATE MOMENTS

#1291 WANTED—Ruth Langan
Devil's Cove

Landscape designer Hannah Brennan was falling fast for her mysterious boss, Ethan Harrison. She'd been hired to turn around the gardens of his Devil's Cove mansion, and instead she found herself planting smiles on the face of this grieving widower. Yet when unexplained accidents threaten Hannah's life, would she trust him to tell her the truth about his past—and their future?

#1292 AN ORDER OF PROTECTION—Kathleen Creighton
Starrs of the West

Policeman Scott Cavanaugh couldn't help but be the hero to his partner's sister Joy Lynn Starr. Even though he had plenty of reasons not to trust this damsel-in-distress, he found himself believing her story that something terrible had befallen her roommate. Now in a desperate search for the truth, Scott must stop a kidnapper from grabbing the one woman he's come to cherish above all others.

#1293 JOINT FORCES—Catherine Mann
Wingmen Warriors

After being held prisoner in a war-torn country, Sergeant J. T. "Tag" Price returned home to find his marriage nearly over—until his wife, Rena, dropped a bomb of her own. She was pregnant! As he set out to romance his wife again, sudden danger loomed—someone wanted him and his family dead. Now he had to fight against this perilous foe to save his wife and unborn child...

#1294 MANHUNT—Carla Cassidy
Cherokee Corners

FBI agent Nick Mead sensed his witness Alyssa Whitefeather wasn't telling him everything she knew about the serial killer he was trying to catch. He needed to convince this Native American beauty that she could trust him with her life—and her secrets. Alyssa wanted to tell Nick about her visions of the murderer, but what would he say when he learned the next victim was *him?*

#1295 AGAINST THE WALL—Lyn Stone
Special Ops

There was something about Maggie Mann that made scientist Rick Dornier stand up and take notice. She wasn't strictly beautiful, but she stirred his blood and proved to be a real challenge. Rick had been determined to find out what Maggie knew about his missing sister, but would his feelings for her prove to be the deadliest distraction of all...?

#1296 DEAD AIM—Anne Woodard

One minute Dr. Solange Micheaux was tending to injured patients. The next, she was on the run with Special Agent Jack Mercier in a deadly race against time. She'd been in the wrong place at the wrong time, and Jack had no choice but to take her with him. But as the hours ticked down, Solange became critical to his success—even though each passion-filled moment they shared could be their last.

SIMCNM0404